THE COWBOY FALLS FOR THE VETERINARIAN

MILLER BROTHERS OF TEXAS BOOK THREE

NATALIE DEAN

DEDICATION

*I'd like to dedicate this book to YOU! The readers of my books.
Without your interest in reading these heartwarming stories of love,
I wouldn't have made it this far. So thank you so much for taking the
time to read any and hopefully all of my books.*

*And I can't leave out my wonderful mother, son, sister, and Auntie. I
love you all, and thank you for helping me make this happen.*

Most of all, I thank God for blessing me on this endeavor.

OTHER BOOKS BY NATALIE DEAN

CONTEMPORARY ROMANCE

Miller Family Saga

BROTHERS OF MILLER RANCH
Miller Family Saga Series 1
Her Second Chance Cowboy

Saving Her Cowboy

Her Rival Cowboy

Her Fake-Fiance Cowboy Protector

Taming Her Cowboy Billionaire

Brothers of Miller Ranch Complete Collection

MILLER BROTHERS OF TEXAS
Miller Family Saga Series 2
The New Cowboy at Miller Ranch Prologue

Humbling Her Cowboy

In Debt to the Cowboy

The Cowboy Falls for the Veterinarian

Almost Fired by the Cowboy

Faking a Date with Her Cowboy Boss

Miller Brothers of Texas Complete Collection

BRIDES OF MILLER RANCH, N.M.

Miller Family Saga Series 3

Cowgirl Fallin' for the Single Dad

Cowgirl Fallin' for the Ranch Hand

Cowgirl Fallin' for the Neighbor

Cowgirl Fallin' for the Miller Brother

Cowgirl Fallin' for Her Best Friend's Brother

Cowboy Fallin' in Love Again

Brides of Miller Ranch Complete Collection

Miller Family Wrap-up Story

(An update on all your favorite characters!)

❧

Copper Creek Romances

BAKER BROTHERS OF COPPER CREEK

Copper Creek Romances Series 1

Cowboys & Protective Ways

Cowboys & Crushes

Cowboys & Christmas Kisses

Cowboys & Broken Hearts

Cowboys & Second Chances

Cowboys & Wedding Woes

Cowboys' Mom Finds Love

Baker Brothers of Copper Creek Complete Collection

CALLAHANS OF COPPER CREEK

Though I try to keep this list updated in each book, you may also visit my website nataliedeanauthor.com for the most up to date information on my book list.

CONTENTS

1

***

Sterling

Sterling stood in one of the fields on his family's expansive ranch. He double-checked the reading he had written down for the latest pH soil test in the purple-flag area. Good to go. This time, he hadn't switched the nine to a six, like he was often wont to do. When he was satisfied that he had recorded it in his notebook correctly, he was tempted to just call it a day and head back to the manor. But then he remembered that Solomon and Frenchie were meeting with their wedding planner back at home. Staying right where he was in this patch of field suddenly seemed like a much better idea.

It wasn't that he resented his older brother, he didn't. If anyone deserved a sweet lady on his arm, it was Solomon. It was just that with his eldest two brothers engaged and his twin getting serious with Teddy, Sterling couldn't help but feel a bit... outdone.

He shook his head, his dark hair moving about. He'd taken to growing it out, trying to separate himself a bit more from Silas, his twin brother, but the reactions were mixed. Most seemed not to notice at all, and his mother wanted him to cut it. But he just needed *something*. He felt like he was being left behind, permanently fixed in the shadows of his older brothers.

No one wanted to be the worse twin, but that was what Sterling was.

Unless he could conclude his experiment and potentially end up earning his family more money to add to their billions.

Alright, he was getting ahead of himself, but he was pleased with the information he was gathering so far. Sure, his brother Silas had really gotten into the manual labor aspect of the ranch and was always off fixing something, or learning this, or doing that, but those projects were mostly all for vanity's sake. They had handymen, experts that could handle that. But what Sterling was doing? Well, that required a real expert.

...or a layman with a lot of time and money on his hands.

Because even though his family cycled their crops like they were supposed to, their output was middling at best. Sterling's father never seemed to care much; after all, they were a ranch, not a farm, but Sterling knew that a boost of only a few percent could yield a healthy profit bump.

And that was what dear ol' Dad was always going on about, right? Maximizing profits? There was only so much blood his family could squeeze out of a stone, but what if Sterling found a whole new stone entirely? A stone that they could *build* on.

Granted, that was if he could collect enough data to understand what was lackluster about their soil and finish concocting his own feed mix to replenish whatever that was. And if his feed worked, well then that too was another thing to package up and sell. It would be a two-pronged measure of success, and then he wouldn't be sliding by anymore. Who knew, with the tension between Dad and Sterling's older siblings, maybe he'd end up as the new favorite.

That would be something, wouldn't it? Growing up, it hadn't really mattered that Sterling had maintained a perfect 4.0 in all of his classes. It hadn't mattered that he was one of the best swimmers, best shot-putters, and best wrestlers for his weight class. Oh sure, all of those things were *expected* of him, but they were just jewels on the crown. Because Sterling was doomed to be the fourth son in six, and there wasn't much for him to do besides "not mess up" his family's reputation or legacy.

"Well, at least I'm not Samuel," he muttered to himself, tucking his notebook away in his leather satchel and moseying back to his truck. Poor Samuel had had the misfortune of being born a little too soft, a little too sweet. It was like the guy hadn't inherited any of his father's business-shark senses, and that left him out in the cold. The black sheep. Sterling was glad that his eldest brother was off making his own life on their aunt and uncle's ranch. But running away wasn't an option for Sterling.

Sterling was a lot of things, but a coward wasn't one of them.

Besides, his timing couldn't be much better considering Solomon and Dad were barely talking, and Silas was about to refuse to be a go-between for them anymore. All Sterling had to do was figure out his little experiment.

But considering he had already collected his samples for the day and checked his other reading spots, there wasn't much left to do in his fields. Adjusting the strap of his satchel, he headed back towards where he had parked his truck.

He supposed he hadn't thought that part through and had

left his ride all the way back at the beginning of his strip of work, by the pigpens.

Sterling hated the pigpens.

First of all, they smelled terrible. Second of all, they were incredibly noisy. He wasn't sure where he had ever gotten the idea that the creatures were relatively quiet, but they most definitely were *not*. Even remotely. Plus, there were always several workers monkeying around with things, and Sterling always felt like he was in the way.

They never said anything to him, of course, but he could feel it. No one wanted the owner's son around while they were workshopping things. And they were definitely workshopping, since the pigs weren't even close to one of the Miller's staple crops. Apparently, there were still all sorts of kinks that needed to be worked out with the animals. From pen configurations to feeding schedules and even their breeding program. Most of the time, Sterling's eyes would just glaze over when the workers went into the things they needed to improve.

But as he walked past, he couldn't help but notice one of the pigs standing right at the edge of the pen and staring at him. He gave her a little wave, and her head jerked up and down while she grunted.

"Is that so?" he asked her, pausing long enough for her to get in several more grunts. She was a big ol' sow, with a healthy pink hide and bright eyes. The bright rainbow tag in her ear told him that she was Peggy—because Mom wasn't always the most creative when it came to names—and if he recalled right, she had an attitude.

Almost as if she heard his thoughts, she let out another round of grunts and exclamations, really giving Sterling the what-have-you. He couldn't help but chuckle, amused by her personality. He remembered reading once that pigs were incredibly intelligent, which was easier to believe with the way Peggy was looking at him.

"You know, none of the boy pigs are gonna wanna kiss you with that kinda mouth on you," he teased, walking towards her. He'd seen some of the workers scratch under her chin before, so he wondered if she would allow him the honor.

He didn't quite make it there, however, as his phone started to ring in his pocket. The only people who ever called him on his personal number were family members, so he answered without thinking about it.

"Hey Sterling, are you at the manor right now?"

He recognized the voice of his younger brother, Sal. Although many folks always thought he was older because of his sheer size. "Yeah. I'm out by the pens right now, just finished up in the fields. You need something?"

His brother sighed. "Yeah, I had this package that I meant to send to our PO box, but it accidentally got sent to our real address. Do you mind driving down to the main road to our mailbox and grabbing it?"

"What, shipping more contraband to our house?"

"You're hilarious. If you must know, it's custom hot sauce from Hawaii."

"Why do you need custom hot sauce from Hawaii?"

"Um, do I interrogate you about your packages?"

"You know full well you would if I was asking you to pick it up."

"Alright. Fair enough. But seriously, do you mind? You know how people like to drive by and mess with things."

He did know. Their mailbox was all the way at the end of their drive, connected to the main road. It was big, almost like a safe, but it didn't stop people from driving by and hitting it with baseball bats or dropping a firecracker inside. Nothing had happened in the last six months, but one never knew, so his family had taken to a more secure PO box in the city.

"Yeah, I'll head home and grab the keys. I assume you're calling me because it's already been delivered and isn't just on its way?"

"You got it."

"Alright. I'll see you later, brother."

"Um yeah, maybe. I'm kinda dealing with something down in the southern edge of the business district right now."

"Really? I haven't heard of anything."

"Just something on my own. Thanks again, brother. We'll talk later."

"Yeah, we will."

Then the call ended. Sterling felt a lick of curiosity at what his younger brother could be up to, but in the end shrugged it off. Sal was salivating to be someone in the family even more than Sterling was, and if he was up to something, it was best to just wait and see what it was.

Besides, Sal was all muscle and insecurity, constantly pining after their father's attention. Sterling wasn't like that.

Not at all.

2

Elizabeth

*E*lizabeth was not having a great day.

In fact, one could almost say that she was having a no good, dirty-rotten, awful, very *bad* day.

She'd had no idea that it was going to be so terrible when she had woken up. If she had, she would have turned right around and crawled back into bed. But *noooo*, she'd gone out completely oblivious to all the awful that was waiting for her.

Only to promptly be let go from the veterinary practice she had been working at. Not as a vet, of course, but as an *assistant* veterinarian. She hadn't been given a solid reason either, if only because they all knew the real reason, they were deciding to part ways.

Because the truth was, Elizabeth had a real issue of arguing with the vet about what was the best procedure to do or the best method of care.

But how could she *not*? The head of the practice was almost seventy years old and as stubborn as could be. One of those old, *old*-fashioned types who asked her why she didn't want to get married and told her that she spoke "white." He also kept using outdated procedures, which often caused the animals they were supposed to be helping to be in unnecessary pain or lengthen their healing time.

"Office politics," she grumbled to herself, pressing the pedal to the metal perhaps a *bit* harder than she should have. But all she wanted to do was get home, draw herself a bath, and soak away some of her troubles. Maybe some chamomile bath salts? Or even eucalyptus? Elizabeth had never really been into makeup or beauty products, but she had always loved her bath enhancements.

Granted, she really couldn't afford a ticket at the moment, so maybe slowing down would be her best bet. Her eyes slid over to her stack of mail that she had thrown into her front seat after hurrying into the city that morning, most of them being bills that were almost due or just past.

She hated how long her commute was. An hour and forty minutes between the city and the small town she lived in was going to kill her car, but it was one of the only places she could find a job. Apparently, most of the vet practices in the area were family affairs, employing children, nieces, and nephews. They didn't want a freshly graduated student who they didn't know from Adam.

She just needed some time to save up. To get out from under the student loans that were crushing her and catch up on her other bills. Namely her phone. She couldn't let that get shut off.

Except... now she had no job. She was unemployed. Sure,

she could maybe collect a little unemployment, but she was sure her former bosses would fight her on it.

Ugh.

It felt like everything was mounting up on her, and no matter how hard she tried to be responsible, she was always a step behind.

It wouldn't do her any good to work herself into a frenzy while she was stuck on her long commute. She needed to take a deep breath, calm down, and let herself focus on the things that she *could* fix at the moment.

Her hand went to the radio, her MP3 player already plugged into the aux cord. She'd had the thing since high school, and it'd certainly gotten her through plenty of awful times. But just when she was about to hit play on the thing, a sputtering sound caught her attention, quickly growing in volume until her car was suddenly slowing down.

"Oh no," she groaned to herself, her blood running cold. "No, no, *no*, this cannot be happening!"

Oh, but it was. Her car continued rumbling, continued slowing, and she barely managed to pull it over to the side of the road before it stopped entirely, smoke billowing from under its hood.

"Not good," she said, shaking her head.

She wanted to say more. Oh, she wanted to say a whole *lot* more, but that wouldn't get her anywhere either. She needed to gather the facts of her situation and figure out what to do. She could worry about the peripherals later.

Well, at least she had friends with cars. Reaching for her purse in the backseat, she pulled out her cell phone. Only to remember that it had died back when she had been talking to a college friend, Tyra, after being let go. And it had died because her car charger had stopped working that morning.

Yeah, definitely a horrible day.

Well, she wasn't helpless. It was still early in the morning and she hadn't been driving for long, so it was probably just a few hours' walk back to the city. Once she got there, she could get her phone charged and arrange for a tow from *someone.*

And maybe she would luck out, run into someone before then. It was unlikely, but if not, she'd get some good cardio in.

"Alright, you've been through worse. This is just another inconvenience, not a tragedy." Besides, it was going to make her bath *really* nice.

Elizabeth went to her trunk, grabbing her sunscreen, a water bottle and an emergency flare. As a vet, she always taught herself to be prepared just in case. She'd heard horror stories of people being stranded or lost and not making it because of a lack of supplies, so she wasn't going to let that happen to her.

Still, even though she told herself to focus on the doable and ignore everything else, she couldn't help but grumble to herself as she started to hoof it down the road. At least she was wearing comfortable shoes, considering she'd been planning for a ten-hour shift of helping animals, and her sunscreen was a wonderful mix of coconut and that special smell that could only be described as "summer."

"Just think of it as a workout. This is like... a free gym class that you normally would have had to pay a guest fee for."

That almost worked, but not quite. On second thought, she headed back to the front of her car, grabbed her MP3 player and headphones, then locked everything up so she could head off.

Her music plus the active task of applying her sunscreen to wherever she had skin exposed helped the time go by faster. It didn't hurt that she was actually in a pretty part of the state, with tall, lush fields on either side of the road. To her right was corn, waving and reedy in the bright sun, their golden tassels like little fireworks at the ends. To her left was tall, thick green grass. Or maybe it was wheat. She didn't really know, but she didn't need to in order to recognize the beauty of it. Much further south, and there wouldn't have been enough moisture and far too much heat for those plants. Further north, and it would have been different crops entirely. Or... maybe it was something about different growing seasons? She actually wasn't sure on that part.

But still, she enjoyed the greenery on both sides, swishing gently in the breeze, offering her the slightest shade from the sun as it beat down on the heated road. It was one of the few actually tarred and maintained paths, which she guessed was because it cut across most of the state. At least she knew it wasn't potholes or giant rocks in the road that had ended her car's life.

The sun, for as strong as it liked to beat down, was pretty too, making the road shimmer in rippling golds and blues. It wasn't as hot as it could be, and with the breeze it was almost pleasant, especially with water to drink whenever she grew warm. Far from some of the blistering days they got in Texas.

Yeah, it could be a lot worse. Then again, she wasn't sure that she wanted to tempt fate by thinking that. She didn't even want to know what else it might try to pile on top of her. At least she was single, so she couldn't be broken up with.

But as she was musing, she saw the faintest blip of a shadow up ahead. A moment later, the figure solidified, and she realized it was a human! A real human!

Elizabeth couldn't believe it. She'd only been walking for fifteen minutes and she'd actually found somebody! It seemed too good to be true, and yet there they were, beside a truck and some sort of large safe-like thing.

She took a couple more steps forward before realizing it was a man. And a tall one at that, with broad shoulders that cut a dynamic silhouette in the stark sunlight. That made her hesitate for a moment, because how many horror movies had she seen that had started with a stranger running into another stranger on a long strip of road.

It wasn't like she was a terribly suspicious person, but she was a single woman in the middle of nowhere with no phone and nothing but an emergency flare in her hand. At least she was six feet tall. Although she wasn't beefy or cut like a warrior, she had always been a nicely muscled woman. Her father had always joked that it had been all the books she'd carried in her backpack as a kid. Goodness knew she didn't have any time for sports with her busy academic schedule.

But hey, she'd graduated high school a year early with a full semester of college credits, so clearly all the back pain had been worth it.

She took one more long glance at the figure, whose back was to her, before deciding. It was worth the risk, if only to get her home faster and to her wonderful bath.

"Hey!" she called, waving her arms. "Hey, excuse me, sir!"

She would just have to hope her luck turned around.

3

Sterling

*W*as there someone calling to him?

Sterling looked up from the mail he was sorting through, pausing to listen more carefully. Sure enough, he heard a voice again, definitely human and definitely trying to catch his attention.

Surprised, he turned towards the sound to see a woman striding confidently towards him, her steps long and assured. She was still a way off, but he could make out enough of her features to tell that she was pretty—and also very determined-looking.

He tensed automatically, because normally someone striding towards him like that meant trouble, but he relaxed quickly. He wasn't at a bar or at a business function where things were tense. They were just on a road, and she was a single person with nothing on her. The chances that she was a threat were slim to none.

She slowed as she grew closer, as if she suddenly realized that she should be cautious. She had a friendly expression across her features when she eventually stopped, and he was surprised to see just how tall she was.

"Hey there. Not exactly the season for hiking enthusiasts," he said, affixing her with one of his grins. Silas always said it was his soap opera smolder, but Sterling thought it was just a pleasant sort of grin.

But she didn't seem amused in the slightest. "Actually, my car broke down about a fifteen-minute walk back there. I was hoping to run into someone who could take me to the city so I can get a tow and charge my phone."

Oh, no wonder she hadn't been in the mood to blush or flirt. He couldn't blame her. But still, a fifteen-minute walk by herself was a pretty brave thing to do, especially considering she was about in the middle of nowhere.

"What, were you going to walk all the way back to the city?"

Her dark, dark eyes affixed him with a look that seemed to stare right through to the very core of him. Her eyes were lined in thick lashes, making her umber gaze that much more intense. It almost made his breath catch, but he managed to hide it in a cough. Well... mostly hide it.

"That was the plan. But now that we've run into each other, I'm hoping that you might be willin' to help? Maybe charge my phone if you got a car cord? Or let me sit in the AC of your truck while I wait for one of my friends?"

Sterling smiled broadly. "Well, I'm sure I can help with that. You can charge your phone while I drive you to the city. In fact, I know a pretty good mechanic shop that could probably tow you up right pretty."

Her face brightened at that, and while he had noticed she was pretty before, he hadn't realized just how *beautiful* she was. Her features were broad and smooth, a red undertone to her skin that almost made the sunlight bounce golden off of her dark complexion. "Really? That's a lot to ask."

"Well, that's why I'm offering." He tried to make sure his smile looked charitable and not predatory. He knew there were plenty of folks who would want to take advantage of a girl in her situation. He wasn't someone like that at all, but she had no way of knowing that.

Nah, he wasn't interested in being perverted or anything like that. But he was real interested in doing something that would unequivocally help someone for no personal gain.

Because his twin Silas was always called such a *saint* for helping out Teddy and her family. And Frenchie always spoke about how his older brother Solomon practically saved her in her time of need. If Sterling could do something nice for someone who so clearly was a little down on their luck, maybe then he wouldn't be so buried in his brothers' shadows that he couldn't even see the sun.

"Here, why don't we charge your phone first and I'll give my mechanic friend a call. I think you'd like her; she's a smart cookie."

The woman clearly looked surprised by his comment. "The mechanic you know is a woman?"

"Yeah, why? That a strange thing?" He knew perfectly well that it was. Teddy had plenty of stories of sexist and stupid things that had been said to her as a female auto specialist. But his reply was enough to surprise her, and her laugh revealed bright, white teeth behind her full lips.

"Maybe a little. But yeah, that would be nice."

"Alright, well let me hook you up with the charger while I give Teddy a ring."

She nodded, and he made sure to give her space as he walked around to the driver's side of his truck. Although he'd never had a sister, he wasn't an idiot. He knew enough about women that someone who was bigger and taller should respect their personal bubble.

It didn't take long to get Teddy's number up and call it. She was one of about fifteen people in his contacts, and he still spoke to her somewhat on the regular.

Granted, it had been much more on the regular when he had first met her, and she was working on the ranch. She'd had an easy smile and interesting hair, and most of all he'd seen how Silas looked at her. Naturally, if his older brother was mooning over a girl, she had to be something special, so sue Sterling that he'd started flirting with her too.

Not that it was an imposition. She had a backside that most of the current pop artists would dedicate full albums to— although they would never *actually* date someone that size— and a snappy wit that could keep up with both him and his brother. But, for some reason, she'd chosen Silas, and now the two of them were thick as thieves. It wasn't that Sterling *resented* his twin, but he couldn't help but feel like his brother always got everything. As the older twin, he got the responsibility of acquisitions. He got the girl. Heck, when people confused them, they always thought only Silas existed. Not once had his older brother been mistaken for *Sterling*.

Which was crazy considering the massive scarring Silas had along one of his collar bones and going down into his torso. It was from an accident when they were kids—an accident that was *Sterling's* fault—but the guy was majorly self-conscious about it. It was one of the few things that was imperfect about perfect *Silas*.

Although it did seem lately that those imperfect things were growing, more and more fights happening between the older brothers and Sterling. Who knew, with the way things were going, maybe he would end up the new heir of the family instead of just the pointless middle child and younger twin.

"Hey Sterling, long time no ring." He couldn't help but grin a bit impishly at Teddy's casual tone on the phone. He remembered there was a time where she had to hold him at arm's length because things were weird between them. While he was glad that was over, he knew it was only because she and Silas were so rooted in their relationship that they weren't going anywhere. He'd even seen his brother looking at rings online.

"Hey, yeah, it's been busy with you hogging up all my brother's time."

"I ain't takin' any time he don't wanna give. Trust me."

"Yeah, yeah. It's unbecoming to brag, you know."

"Fair 'nuff. Did you need something?"

"Yeah, actually, I have a driver here whose car happened to give out on the road by our estate. Think you could take a look at it?"

"Hold on. Let me check." There was the always amusing sound of Teddy yelling through the shop, her brother yelling back that he couldn't understand her yelling, and then the receptionist guy calling out from the office. After that cacophony of a verbal onslaught finished, Teddy returned to the phone as calm and steady as usual.

"Yeah, we got a tow truck free, but it's probably going to take me at least an hour and a half to get out there. Can you tell me what happened?"

He handed the phone to the woman in his car, who explained the situation and *wow*, it did sound pretty bad. Teddy said something else on the phone and then hit the speaker button.

"Can you hear me?" Teddy asked.

"When *can't* I hear you?" Sterling said.

"Bless your heart, you're just hilarious, aren't you? Anyways, if it's what I'm thinking it is, we can prob'ly fix it by tomorrow afternoon, but I definitely recommend staying in a hotel in the city for the night, ma'am."

The woman looked to Sterling uncertainly. "Are you willing to wait with me here? You don't have to."

"I'm not going to leave you stranded here for an hour and a half. Besides, if I recall right, one of the tows doesn't have AC, right, Teddy?"

He could hear Teddy rolling her eyes, he was sure of it. "How is it that even though you boys have a whole empire to run, you can still remember that one of our trucks doesn't have air conditioning?"

"Answer the question."

"... yeah, it's the broken one. If you can give your friend a ride to the city, I'm sure she'd much appreciate it," Teddy said.

"Alright, then. Maybe I'll swing by your shop and say hi."

"As long as you don't flirt with the new mechanic again."

He chuckled. Her shop had hired a new worker due to an increase in their business with the community center and all. She was a nice enough person, but mostly he did it because it was fun rather than any actual attraction.

"Why? Are you jealous, Teddy?"

"No, she's just easily distractible, and I'm not on your dime anymore, so stop costing me money."

"Ouch, and here I thought we got something special," Sterling said in a teasing tone.

The woman in his passenger seat was giving him a *look*. It wasn't one he had a name for, but it was certainly one that let him know that she was observing every single word they said.

"We do. You're the incorrigible younger twin of my boyfriend, and for some reason, I tolerate your shenanigans. See you soon, Sterling."

"See you soon, Teddy."

She hung up, and he looked to the woman in his passenger seat. "Well, you ready—uh... actually. I don't think I caught your name."

"Elizabeth," she said, offering her hand. "Elizabeth Brown."

"Sterling Miller, nice to meet you L—"

"Don't call me Lizzy," she said quickly as he shook her hand.

"I wasn't going to."

She narrowed her dark eyes at him ever so slightly. "Yes, you were."

He smiled crookedly at that. "Alright, yeah I was. You caught me."

"After thirty years, I've learned enough to recognize the sound of someone even *thinking* it."

"Thirty years?" Sterling couldn't quite help his reaction. The woman looked *young*. Like maybe she was fresh out of college or halfway through it. He wouldn't have guessed over twenty-four.

"You might have heard this before, but black don't crack."

A laugh forced its way out of his mouth at that. That phrase was possibly the last thing that he had expected and certainly wasn't something that was said often around his home. "I might have heard that once or twice before." He collected himself and started the truck. "Do you have a hotel preference?"

Before she could answer, his phone started ringing loudly

with his business tone. The one he specifically gave the workers if there was an emergency. Normally they would contact Solomon or Silas, so if they were reaching out to him, then it *really* had to be something serious.

"Sorry, just one moment," he told Elizabeth, answering quickly.

"What's going on?" Sterling asked the caller.

"Hey, I'm sorry to bother you, boss, but we got a big problem here."

"I figured as much. Equipment malfunction?" Hopefully it wasn't another injury. They were about four months without an accident, and they needed to get to at least six months before their insurance would go down.

"No, nothing like that. It's Peggy."

"Okay... what about Peggy?"

"Well, sir, she's uh... she's..."

"Out with it, I'm in the middle of something."

"Peggy is pregnant."

"I'm sorry, Peggy is what?"

It was only then that Sterling realized he had hit the speaker again out of habit, and his passenger had been listening to everything.

"Lady trouble?" she asked with a wry smile.

"You could say that. Peggy is one of our sows." He turned his attention back to the call. "Peggy is in one of our sow pens, which is only supposed to have *sows* in it, so how on earth is she pregnant? And how do you even know?! She ask for a pregnancy test?"

"Sorry, sir, I don't have any answers for that. I've just come back from being out with the flu. As for her being pregnant, well that's the best guess I've got considering she's trying to give birth right now and having a real bad time of it."

"She *what!?*"

Suddenly the woman in his car straightened. "Take me to her," she said sharply.

Sterling blinked at her. "I'm sorry, what?" He felt like he was repeating himself, but it was already turning out to be quite a day.

"I'm a veterinarian. Take me to Peggy, right now."

What were the chances of that? "Look—"

"I specialize in farm animals, and if you want Peggy to live, I need to get to her as soon as I can. So, start driving!"

It was an order. That much was *very* clear. Sterling didn't like orders, and especially not from strange women that he was helping out. And yet he found himself doing exactly what she said, driving off to the pens again.

4

Elizabeth

When Elizabeth had neared the man, she hadn't expected him to be as handsome as he was. Because he seriously was ridiculously, unfairly handsome. And when he had spoken, his voice had been just like butter. He had the classic sort of cowboy look going for him, but with a whole lot of polish, his hair well maintained even though it was growing out, and he had plenty of muscles. But then all of that went flying out of his very nice truck's window when she heard what sounded like the description of a sow failing to leave the pre-farrowing stage.

It was a dangerous thing to happen, and if not dealt with, it usually resulted in death, for mama and the little ones. Elizabeth wasn't about to let that happen on her watch, even if it was just dumb luck that she was in the right place at the right time.

In her head she was already going through her mental

checklist of what she needed to look for and what she needed to test. She barely noticed their surroundings as the truck flew along a drive then split off to a less polished road, but she did manage to see plenty of high-tech automation, healthy crops and expensive equipment.

That was good. If they had a bunch of money sunk into the place, they were likely to have supplies on hand that she could use. She wished that she had her emergency vet bag, but that had been left in the car because of the long trek to the city she had thought she'd been about to walk.

Sterling pulled up to what obviously had to be the barn, and Elizabeth was opening her door before he even came to a full stop, vaulting out and dashing towards where they had the pigs penned. It was a wide area, which she had expected, but what she hadn't anticipated were nearly a dozen workers standing around while looking completely bewildered.

"Is there a reason why your vet has been delayed in getting here?" she asked the closest one.

"Our vet?" they murmured faintly.

That was *not* a good sign. But Elizabeth didn't let that stop her. Every moment was precious. She kept right on walking towards the nearest door that looked like it led into the pens. She could just hop the fence, but she needed equipment first.

"Where's your medical bag?" she asked the moment she was in. But she was met with more uncertain looks. "You have animals, yes? Then where is the emergency medical bag for when your vet arrives? Surely you have *something!*"

"We have a couple of vets on retainer through a service. They drive in with their full equipment from the city or we transport the livestock to them. Although usually, the animal is just put down if it's going to be in pain."

Elizabeth whipped around to see that the handsome man

had followed her, although he looked a bit perplexed. "Your closest veterinary care is over an hour away and you have *no* emergency supplies? What happens when something... well, something like *this* happens?"

Why was he looking at her like she was bizarre for being keyed up? An animal was in pain and no one knew what to do! When one relied on animals for their living, they owed their livestock respect and caring. And part of that was having a plan for an emergency.

"Like I said, we put the animal down, more often than not. Humanely, of course."

If it were any other situation, Elizabeth would have read him the riot act. But as it were, a sow was in pain with a preventable condition and needed her help.

"*Fine!* I need your human first aid kit. And garbage bags! And if you have any rubbing alcohol, I might even take vodka if you have it." She pointed to one of the workers that looked the muddiest, like he might have been in the pens for a while. "*You.* Lead me to Peggy."

Thankfully no one questioned her. A few scattered, she guessed to get the supplies she asked for, and the one led her into the pens. She was relieved to see that they were heading to a smaller one that was mostly indoors. After the debacle with the bag, she was worried that they wouldn't even have birthing pens.

"She went in there herself?" Elizabeth asked, eyeing the ol' girl. She was lying on her side and breathing heavily, the poor thing, and she wasn't the peachy-pale color one would hope. No, almost ashen. It broke Elizabeth's heart to see her laboring so, and it wasn't going to get better.

In fact, if she didn't get in there, it was going to get a whole lot worse.

"I'm sorry," the handsome man said, coming up behind her.

What was his name again? Silver something?

"But what's going on here again? And why are you using a first aid kit?"

Normally Elizabeth would just brush him off. She hated stupid questions even more than she hated trying to explain her thoughts to other people. It was a waste of time nine out of ten, as usually they didn't understand the terms she needed to use.

"Your pig is going to die unless I help her. If she can't leave the pre-farrowing stage, the birthing won't go anywhere, but her body will fight *real* hard to force things along anyway. It doesn't spell out anything good for the mama or the piglets, and it's incredibly painful." He opened his mouth, and she held up her hand. "If you're going to say anything about putting this creature down for something that is easily treatable while you're within my kicking distance, well I highly recommend you reevaluate your word choice."

His mouth snapped closed.

"Now where is that first aid kit?!" she hollered.

One of the workers came dashing up to her, pushing a small cart. She was relieved to see the first aid kit was more like a first aid trunk, and practically ripped open the top.

Bandages, rubbing alcohol, burn cream, antihistamine cream. That was a good sign. She dug deeper and found what she hoped would be buried towards the bottom, tweezers for splinters and the like then—*Aha!*—there it was. An emergency blade to cut off clothing in case of it getting caught in a machine or pinning someone.

She yanked out the whole package for it and set about ripping it apart. The more time she took, the less of a chance of survival Peggy had. So she needed to work fast.

The rest of the world fell away as she amassed all of her supplies then shoved them into the arms of one of the workers, ordering him to follow her. He did so, and the two of them made their way to the poor girl.

"Hey there," Elizabeth said soothingly as she approached. Pigs were funny creatures. They were whip-smart and kind, but they also could eat *anything.* That led to a very strange dichotomy of them being quite loving and friendly but also able to take off a hand if the mood suited them.

And she'd seen what happened when it *did* suit them, and she certainly didn't want that to be her.

Peggy let out a truly heartbreaking noise, and Elizabeth took a step closer. "Oh sweetie. It sounds like you're in a lot of pain, but I'm here to help. I've done this before, so you don't have to worry; this is practically going to be a breeze."

She knew that some thought it was strange that she talked to the animals like they were human patients, but it worked for her, and it seemed to work for the creatures she helped as well, so she never saw the harm.

"I know you're probably thirsty and more than a bit hungry, but that needs to wait for a little longer, okay?"

Peggy let out a wuffle that would have been adorable in any other situation, but in the current circumstances mostly just seemed very sad. Swallowing hard to keep her emotions down, Elizabeth closed the small distance between them, setting her hand on Peggy's side. She was *way* too warm and probably dehydrated. If she was only back at the vet's office—

She cut off that kind of thought. She wasn't there, and she wasn't going to get Peggy there so better not to waste energy on it. Instead, she poured all the love and warmth into her hands, willing her patient to be able to feel it and be put at ease.

Once she felt that was done, she stepped away and grabbed

the rubbing alcohol then poured all the way along her arms. Then she put on the latex gloves that were inside and poured the rubbing alcohol over her again. Considering that she was going to be working in an unsterile environment—not uncommon with farm animals—she needed to take all the precautions she could.

"Stay here and do everything I say," she said flatly to the worker, her mind already switching into doctor mode.

And in her doctor mode, there was only her and the patient. Turning back to Peggy, she knelt down next to the poor mama-to-be and got to work, murmuring comforts the entire time. It wasn't easy, and Peggy may have clipped her with her back feet once or twice, but after a half-hour of solid work, the sow was going into farrow. That was the biggest roadblock, and for a moment Elizabeth had been worried it was one they wouldn't get over. But they did, well *Peggy* did, and the next thing Elizabeth knew, she was helping Peggy birth piglets.

Oh, they were cute, chunky little things. And only four of them. Strange that a sow would have trouble going into farrow on such a small litter, but she supposed sometimes those things just happened. Then again, when she recalled how little resources there were around, maybe Miss Peggy was doomed from the start.

"You did good, mama," Elizabeth murmured before rising to her feet, her knees protesting painfully. Ugh, she was only just barely thirty; she was too young for her body to hurt the way it did.

"I got you a water," an especially young worker said as she walked out of the pen, holding out a cool bottle.

Elizabeth took it gratefully and gulped it down.

"Make sure you get water and some food real close to Peggy for her to eat when she wants. And call those useless veterinarians that you supposedly have on contract." Stronger language than Elizabeth would normally ever use in a professional setting, but she was right mad. What would have happened if her car hadn't broken down? A poor animal would have died an incredibly painful death and taken all of her babies with her just because her owners were irresponsible.

Elizabeth couldn't be more unimpressed by all the fancy equipment and nice buildings surrounding her. None of it meant anything if the animals were mistreated. Elizabeth ate meat; she was well aware of what went into farming for the sake of food. But she also knew there was a kind and loving and *respectful* way to treat livestock, and then one that was only obsessed with profit. One that treated living creatures like nothing more than dollar signs. And she didn't need a grand tour to know what kind of place she was in.

How foul.

5

Sterling

*W*atching the woman work was something else.

The last thing Sterling had ever expected was for his hitchhiker to basically hijack the pigpens and start ordering everyone about, but that was exactly what she did.

And she didn't seem to have a single qualm doing it either.

Sterling had never seen someone come in and take over a situation like that, then proceed to calm a *very upset* pig which weighed very much more than her, then get coated in all sorts of liquids and waste that no one would want to get covered with. And yet, she didn't even bat an eye.

If he didn't know better, he would think that it was *her* ranch and she'd known Peggy her whole piggy life. And yet, the two had just met. In fact, *he'd* just met the mystery woman too.

What were the chances that the woman stranded in front of their house also happened to be a veterinarian with a specialization in farm animals!? That was the kind of thing that would have Mom fanning her face and claiming that "God is good," but Sterling honestly didn't find God in most of their business enterprise.

She was like a force of nature, this Elizabeth Brown. All of her energy had been focused on the pig. He could practically feel it in the air, despite her completely calm and collected demeanor otherwise. The workers seemed to be caught up in it too, most of them watching her, awestruck.

Sterling was approaching her afterward without even consciously telling himself to do so, watching the dark column of her neck bob as she completely drained the water bottle that had been handed to her. She reminded him of an old story his mother used to tell him, one that stood hazily in the farther parts of his memory. A legend about how forests and rivers and mountains used to be alive with spirit guardians who fiercely protected them. She could be a protector, as covered in filth as she was.

"That was—"

He didn't even get the congratulations out before she turned to him with a look that most *definitely* wasn't a happy one.

"Are you kidding me?" was what she said instead, handing the empty water bottle to a worker who quickly replaced it with another.

"Pardon me?" Sterling asked, blinking at her.

She was using a tone that he wasn't used to hearing. *No one* used that kind of tone on him, not even his parents. It was a combination of disappointment along with a whole bunch of righteous anger, and he had no idea what he could have possibly done to warrant that.

"I said, *are you kidding me*," she repeated. Nope, that look and tone weren't going anywhere, it seemed. "How is it you have a nice car, designer cowboy boots there, a building that would make some ranchers weep, but you don't even have basic care for your animals?"

Wait, what? Not have basic care? Sterling looked around at the wide sow pen, with its watering troughs and the parts that extended both in and out of the barn. "We...don't?" he said finally, trying to catch up.

A lot had happened in the past thirty minutes, in his defense. He went from knight in shining armor of a very attractive but stranded motorist to watching a live birth of a pig that was also getting its life saved, to being dressed down by a woman who looked like she didn't care that he was bigger, taller and richer than her.

Her eyes went wide at his question, but the anger only got worse. Apparently, that was not the right thing to say. "No! It's not! It's not even close! Look, I know that these animals are how you make your money, but if you can't even afford to give them proper care, to respect them for what they give to you, then you shouldn't have them!" Her words picked up speed as she went along and suddenly, it was like someone had shown a light on what was going on.

She cared about the animals.

That shouldn't have been a revelation. She was a vet; of course she had to like animals at least a little. But none of their contracted help ever reacted like *she* was, and he realized there was a difference between their businesslike way of coming in and cleaning up emergencies or putting sick animals down, and Elizabeth's knock-out, knuckle-biting push to make sure they were healthy.

And for some reason, that suddenly seemed very significant.

"Even if you want to take out the fact that it's our God-given responsibility to be good shepherds to his creatures, do you really think neglected animals make good food? That they *taste* great or are nourishing? Even from a greedy, money standpoint, this is unacceptable." She threw her hands up in the air, all passion and heartache under her furrowed brows. He wondered what had happened to her, what she had seen to make her want to fight so hard for animals that most people thought of as stinky and gross.

"And now you're telling me you don't even *know* that you're lacking!?" She looked around at all of the men around her. "None of you know what you're doing, do you? How to treat, feed and take care of these pigs? Huh?" There were a few muttered responses, but most of the workers had conveniently headed somewhere else when her scolding had started. "You really don't. Sweet glory, none of y'all have a clue. It would take a good vet and team of contractors at least a year to go around fixing all of this and making sure your ship is straight. Because I'm willing to bet the rest of your ranch is like this too. Irresponsible, I tell you. *Irresponsible.*"

"Okay," Sterling heard his mouth say as he watched her mouth move. Her lips were so full and such a pretty gradient that he didn't think he'd ever seen before. From dark, umberish brown to a deep sort of pink. The moving colors punctuated her words, drawing him into every syllable they made.

Her tirade paused, and she narrowed her eyes at him. "What do you mean?"

Oh, had he said something? Swallowing, Sterling caught onto the tail end of his thought and just dived right along with it.

"I mean, okay, then do it."

There was that wide-eyed look again, and for the first time she seemed at a loss for words. "Do... *what*?"

It was insane. He knew that. He knew that even as the words left his mouth. But he meant them wholeheartedly. Silas told him that he had a habit of diving into things feet first—which was basically how the whole firecracker accident happened—but what did Silas know? He was off burning through Father's goodwill while running around with a mechanic from the city.

"Fix this place. Make it good for the animals. I want you to do it."

"...you can't be serious."

"I am. You say we need a good vet to tell us what's what, well I'm not seeing any better one around right now. That is, if you think you're up for it?"

There was that narrowed-eyed gaze again, but he could already see her shoulders and back straightening as she rose to his challenge. "This is a paid consultation, of course," she stated rather than asked.

Oh, he liked her chutzpah. He liked it a lot.

"Naturally. I wouldn't dream of having it otherwise."

"Somehow, I doubt that."

Elizabeth

*E*lizabeth rubbed her fingers over the smooth silicone of her phone case, trying to resist the urge to chew on the rubbery-textured material. She didn't do well with sitting still, but she found herself having to as she waited in the reception area of the auto shop, about to pick up her car and then head to her new job.

She couldn't believe it.

It had been only two days ago that she was jobless with a broken-down car, and in just a few moments, she was going to be driving to her brand-new veterinary consultant gig.

She hadn't meant for anything to happen as it did. She certainly hadn't *planned* on saving a sow's life and then yelling at the owner of a massive enterprise. But her heart had gotten in front of her brain, and the next thing she knew, she was hauling out her always-ready soapbox about the treatment of animals.

Oh yeah, she'd googled the Millers once she'd gotten to her hotel room a couple of hours after saving Peggy. It had been one of the workers who had driven her, the same one who had fetched her the water bottles, and she had gotten the feeling that he was kind of afraid of her. Oh well, probably not a bad thing. Whenever she saw people taking advantage of creatures, she usually wanted to deck someone. And when she found out that Mr. Sterling—apparently not *Silver*—and his family were worth literally over a billion dollars, her rage had increased that much more.

They had *so. Much. Money.* She didn't understand why their animals were in less-than-mediocre conditions. She didn't understand how none of them were vets or had one on-premise at all times. There was no animal husbandry that she could see, and that was enough to have her spitting mad.

"Oh, hey there! You're the new vet for the Miller Ranch, right? I'm Teddy."

Elizabeth looked up from the especially chewable corner of her phone case to see a woman standing in the doorway that must have led back to the mechanics' garage.

"Yes, I'm Elizabeth. You heard about that already?" she asked, standing up and crossing to shake the woman's hand. Her grip was as firm as Elizabeth had expected given her broad shoulders and posture, which the vet appreciated. If anyone got what it was like to be a woman in a male-dominated field, it was clearly the mechanic in front of her.

"Well, it helps that I'm dating one of the boys of that family. The grapevine's pretty short there."

"You're uh... dating in that family?"

Despite Elizabeth's best attempt to keep her tone perfectly polite for the woman who was essentially saving her bacon, she clearly didn't do a good job because Teddy let out a soft laugh.

"I know what you're thinking. And yeah, that family is a real trip. Exactly how you'd imagine a bunch of rich types running around. But Solomon and Silas? They're different. They're real good at seeing things from a practical perspective and actually care about more than money."

Oh. That had to cause some interesting family dynamics. "What about Sterling?"

"Ah yeah, that's the one you were lucky to meet. Sterling is... well, he's Sterling." Teddy laughed again, but Elizabeth just held her stare steady. She needed more data. "See, he and my boyfriend are twins, and they have a lot in common. They're both ridiculously smart, real good at reading people and prone to getting antsy when they're bored. Also have a matching pair of insecurity complexes on 'em, thanks to their father."

There was another pause.

"I feel like there's something else you want to say," Elizabeth prompted finally while the woman looked over the paperwork attached to the dirty clipboard in her hands.

"I... alright, woman to woman. Sterling is handsome and smart and witty and *real* good with smooth talk. But he's definitely, I dunno, *hunting* for something, and I'm not sure if anyone should really be that something."

Alarm bells sounded in the back of her head. "You mean he's a predator?"

"Oh no! Nothing like that! I just mean that it's super clear to me that he feels like he's missing something, while denying that he's missing something, so most of the time he focuses his energy on whatever new thing one of his brothers has to see if that fills the hole.

"I know their older brother Solomon turned down an engagement to a woman in a rich family. Val...gado? Vall... something or other. So then Sterling started dating *two* of the sisters. But then he got bored, broke it off with both of them, and that didn't go well either."

"So, he's a cat around the town then?" Elizabeth said. She knew the type. Men who had too much money and power always thought they could get everything and had loose attitudes towards sex.

"No, not that either." She leaned forward, her voice dropping low. "Look, I shouldn't tell you this because it's pretty personal, but Silas told me his brother broke it off with the girls because both of them were pressuring him to be intimate, and he wasn't into it."

"Is he gay?" She knew how hateful some folks could be, and how they liked to use the Bible as their bludgeoning weapon. She never understood that, as it seemed like just about the most un-Jesus thing that a supposed Jesus-follower could do.

"Silas doesn't think so. Sterling just wants to wait, you know. Until he's married and all. Silas is the same way."

That was interesting. Ever since she was young, Elizabeth had been so keyed into becoming a vet that she didn't have time or space for anything else. Especially dating. Naturally, in college most of her friends had convinced her there was something wrong with her, some reason why she didn't want to date or have any romance at all. But that was crazy. She had other priorities. And why waste the time dating when it was more practical and appropriate to wait for the right guy? Besides, waiting for marriage showed she respected herself.

"Right, well anyways, I'm only telling you since you're going to be a woman on the ranch and working in close quarters with them. When I was first there, Sterling sort of set his sights on me—mostly because of some sort of twin rivalry thing. He was never inappropriate and didn't cross any boundaries, but I guess I just wanted you to know because it can be... intimidating having someone like them flirting with you."

"Especially since he's the one that gave me the job."

"Yeah. That's a real wild part, let me tell you. Sterling really only does things for the ranch if his father specifically tells him what to do, so him going out on a limb is right fascinating."

Elizabeth nodded. That was an awful lot of information about her employer, and some of it did feel quite private. And maybe Teddy and Silas didn't really know why Sterling made the choices he did. Elizabeth didn't know why she had such a hard time believing that the handsome, rich man wasn't a real gigolo, but maybe that was because he was both handsome and rich with a voice that slid down her spine like velvet.

"Anyways, I didn't want to stress you out. I just wanted to... I guess give you the sort of scoop I wish I'd had when I first started working there. It was a pretty stressful time of my life, and I sort of built the guys up in my head as these terrible monsters who were trying to take advantage of me."

"And they weren't?"

She shook her head. "I wouldn't be dating one if they were. In fact, I would have probably punched them in their unfairly handsome faces."

Elizabeth chuckled at that. "I wouldn't recommend decking rich people. They don't take kindly to that."

Teddy's grin grew wolfish. "Oh, I *know*. The whole reason I was there was because I tried to pummel a millionaire competitor of theirs into the ground, but my brother got to him first."

Now that gave Elizabeth pause. "You're kidding?"

So many white, pearly teeth were bared in Teddy's smile, and Elizabeth loved it. "I ain't never kidded about that and I don't think I ever will." She reached into her pocket and handed over the lanyard Elizabeth had left with the worker the previous evening. "Anyway, here's your keys. Best of luck on your first day. Make sure you have a big water bottle on you. They've got spigots around and the like, but it takes valuable time to go back and forth between the two, and their mini-fridges are filled up with the tiniest water bottles."

"I know what you mean. I drained one in practically three gulps."

"Ain't that right? It's Texas, what's with the little sixteen-ounce serving?" They shared another laugh, then Teddy was giving a crooked little salute. "I'll have Roman bring the car around. Hopefully I'll see you again for a non-mechanic-related reason."

"Yeah, I wouldn't mind that."

"Me either. Just remember not to fall in love with any of those boys, because I definitely snatched up the best one." Her face grew serious. "And watch out for Sal. He's jonesing for Solomon's old position."

"What do you mean by—"

But Teddy was already through the door into the mechanic shop, the heavy wood entrance swinging closed behind her.

Huh.

Not the best note to end it on, but Elizabeth just shrugged and went about everything she needed to do. Only a bit later, she was in her car and headed to the ranch, following the GPS until she reached the part where Sterling had to give her manual directions.

Because apparently their estate was so large, as was their

enterprise, that she would get hopelessly lost before ever getting near the pens. Elizabeth kept trying to mentally map out how big that exactly must be, but she never was quite able to put together the total acreage. Surely it couldn't be *so* big.

It was.

The first time she'd been on the ranch, she'd been concentrating on getting to Peggy so hard, running through her mental checklists, that she hadn't realized just how long it had taken them to get from point A to point B. So, as she drove through for the first time on her own, she was wryly grateful for the directions.

Elizabeth finally arrived at the pigpens, grabbing her notebook, a pen, and her fancy sort of hip-pack that she put her phone in and clipped her thermos to. It was made of leather, with a belt attachment that went through the loops of her jeans and another strap that buckled around her thigh. It had been something she had salivated over for years but could never justify the cost of it. But then her dad had bought it for her as a graduation present, and she used it whenever she could.

He *shouldn't* have, considering he was on a fixed income and they were both struggling to pay off her mother's funeral. Nevertheless, he must have saved for a couple of months with his part-time grocery job that he was able to keep even though he was retired, and that touched Elizabeth more than he could ever know.

Her father was something else, as lonely as he had been since her mother left the world. He was the one she got her drive from. And with the sudden pay hike she was going to get from the Millers, Elizabeth was already daydreaming of what she could do for him.

But first, the pigs.

She started at one end, walking around and writing everything she spotted that needed work. Improvement. She figured she needed to aim astronomically high in order for Sterling to negotiate her down to something passable. It was a tactic she had learned in high school, and it served her well into adulthood.

Except when it came to stubborn old veterinarians who needed to retire, it seemed.

"What do you think?" she asked the closest pig. She didn't have to worry about any humans misinterpreting and thinking she was talking to them, because there wasn't a single worker around as far as she could tell.

Maybe they were hiding, scared of her after her first display there. Oh well, all the better for her.

"Maybe some traffic cones? And some buried logs for rooting? Yeah, you'd like that, wouldn't you beautiful? Something for you to not be bored, huh?" Elizabeth reached over the part of the fence she was inspecting, scratching the top of the pig's head. The poor girl had bite marks on her ears and tail, which was a classic sign of some *very* bored and frustrated animals.

So many people didn't get how smart pigs were, and without the proper enrichment, they turned destructive. Pigs loved to chew and needed both hard things and soft, destroyable things.

"And how about some feed balls too? Some salt licks? Would you like that? I bet you would like that, wouldn't you gorgeous? Well, you just give me your opinion whenever you got it, okay?"

The sow gave some appreciative grunts, and Elizabeth couldn't help but wonder if she was the only one who ever talked to these animals. How sad. She wondered if she could add human interaction to her list. Sure, the animals were going to end up as food, but that didn't mean they had to be treated

like factory by-products. They deserved care, respect and gratitude for everything they would provide.

"Don't worry. I'm gonna fight for you guys, okay?"

Elizabeth gave herself a nod and continued to move along.
Of course, her progress would go faster if she didn't stop to ask
most of the curious hogs how they were and give them some
solid chin scratches, but she wasn't going to *not* chat considering the complete lack of enrichment around them.

She had made it into the interior of the barn when she
heard a pair of assured footsteps behind her. Turning, she saw
Sterling, but was surprised to see an almost exact copy of
him too.

Huh, she had heard that they were twins, but she hadn't
expected them to be identical. And they certainly were, all
strong jawlines and intense gazes that probably intimidated a
good number of people.

Sure, there were slight differences between them. Sterling's
hair was clearly grown a bit more, forming a gentle, casual
wave across the top of his head, and he had about ten or so
more pounds of muscle on him. But other than that, it was
clear that when God made one of them, he decided he did such
a good job on the package that he needed to make it twice.

"Hey there. I see you're already hard at work. Can't say I'm
surprised though." Sterling affixed her with a *dazzler* of a smile,
and if Elizabeth still wasn't so latently angry about the pig situation, she might have been moved by it.

Or maybe swoon was a better word for it. But either way,
she let it wash over her and moved right along. Men could be
pretty sometimes, sure, but it wasn't something to get worked
up over when she had so much on her plate.

"I'm making a list of everything that needs to be improved
or completely redone."

"Wait, what's going on?" the other said, which had to be Silas going by what Teddy had said earlier. "You're planning renovations? Does Dad know you're taking another project under your wing? Is the soil one even wrapped up?"

Elizabeth watched Sterling's face as he answered. Strangely enough, he looked a little uncomfortable. That was interesting. But the man just shrugged, making a dismissed gesture. "You and Solomon aren't the only ones who have ambition. Let's just say I saw an opportunity and I took it."

Oh... less interesting. Elizabeth rolled her eyes and returned to her inspection. It seemed that his interest in the pigs was just some sort of rich sibling rivalry pettiness. Wealthy family drama was something for prime-time television, not her working hours. Besides, all she cared about was whether the pigs were getting the better end of the stick, and if things worked out like they had all agreed, they would.

The two brothers continued to talk, Silas asking questions and Sterling giving non-answers. The older twin wasn't being aggressive, as far as she could tell with what little attention she was sparing for them. He was just curious. But Sterling was clearly *not* about it. He kept giving half or non-answers, clearly trying to have the subject die. Eventually, Elizabeth *almost* felt bad for him and she found herself asking a question in a flat tone, interrupting their not-really-a-conversation.

"So, who do I need to speak to about setting up direct deposit and my benefits?"

The two blinked at her, as if they had forgotten that she was there entirely. It was Silas who answered.

"That would be Solomon, actually. He's up in his office now, so if you'd like, and you have the necessary info, I'd be happy to take you there."

"Thank you. I hate paperwork, so it'll be nice to get it out of the way."

There, she had done her good deed for the day. As a thank-you for paying her double the going rate for a recently graduated vet. But that was it. If he wanted to get on her good side, he had to do right by all the animals first.

7

Sterling

"I guess I just don't get what you think you're doing," Silas said.

Sterling just stared at his twin, who was leaning up against the counter, trying to look nonchalant but appearing anything but. Yeah, maybe he should have thought of an explanation for Elizabeth once his family found out about her, but he'd thought he had more time. Not her first day on the job. Besides, he wasn't even sure if she was going to stick around.

And yet she had, and at the end of the workday, she'd promised him her report would be in his email before she went to sleep that night. And that he could expect another the next day. And the next until she was finished assessing the pens and at that point, they would decide if they wanted to move on to other animal habitats on the ranch.

To be perfectly honest, Sterling hadn't thought that far

ahead. He hadn't taken the time to figure out how they were going to budget the salary he had offered her. Which, as it turns out, had been on the generous side. His father would be even *more* peeved if he found out one of his middle sons was overpaying. Sterling didn't do it purposefully. He'd been relatively sure that he was lowballing her when he'd offered her what would work out to be around eighty-eight thousand or so if she ended up lasting a whole year—which seemed about as possible as pigs flying and the south giving up their sweet tea. But apparently, about seventy-five thousand was the average for a farm veterinarian. Then there was all the costs of the repairs and "enrichment" that were going to be in her report.

So yeah, maybe he should have thought things through a little more, but that wasn't any reason for Silas to stand there and *lecture* him like he was stupid.

"Good thing you don't need to then, huh? You can worry yourself with the community center and whatever you're planning to surprise Teddy."

"Who says I'm planning a surprise for Teddy?"

Sterling affixed his brother with a look. "You're my twin. I can tell these things."

Silas flushed, unable to hold in his emotions as usual. That was the reason that Solomon had been supposed to be the inheritor of the empire even though Silas was brilliant at acquisitions and understanding financial trends. The second oldest was often as cool as a cucumber while the elder twin had the worst poker face.

"Stop trying to change the subject. We're talking about you and this veterinarian you randomly hired as a contractor."

"Why are you making such a stink about it? Usually you can't be bothered with what I'm doing. Haven't you spent the last few months practically chasing me away?"

"Of course, you'd call it that when you kept insisting on making Teddy uncomfortable."

"Uncomfortable, huh? Yeah, because I'm *such* a predator, we know that. Just because you're too awkward to banter with the girl that you're madly in love with doesn't mean that I'm a bad guy for doing so."

"You are so frustrating, Sterling. I don't think you're a bad guy. You're my twin! I just... I just don't *get* you sometimes."

"What's to get? I'm not like a soil experiment. I'm your *brother*. And, I might add, a grown man." He could tell that Silas was gearing up to say something else, to explain himself maybe, but he was so very done. He was done with the entire *day*. But instead of more lecturing, his older brother just sighed.

"I'm glad that you're taking more interest in the ranch again. I think it would do us all some good to, you know, go back to how things were when we were younger."

"Things have always been this way, Silas. We just didn't realize it until we were old enough to be bought into the business."

"...maybe."

He didn't say anything after that, and Sterling took it as his cue to leave. He was irritated and the end of his nerves felt more than frazzled. He wasn't used to flying by the seat of his pants. Of all of his brothers, he was probably the least ambitious and wasn't used to having to juggle so many of his own plans all at once. After all, he was a middle son and a younger twin. What else was there for him to do other than public events, where he was assumed to be Silas at anyway?

As he reached his room, that dissatisfied, malcontented feeling wouldn't go away. He felt like he was still arguing with his brother, which was irritating in the absolute worst way.

When he tried to settle, maybe surf the internet, that energy just wouldn't dissipate.

Oh well. Maybe it was a good time for a workout.

That seemed better than nothing, so he went to the small gym room in the wing he and Silas shared. It wasn't as big as in the main wing or in Sal's, but it had a television, treadmill, elliptical, weight set and a few other machines that were more than enough for him. Besides, he didn't really want to see anyone else at the moment. Just him and his thoughts.

He thought about going and taking one of their horses out for a ride, something he'd taken to doing with Silas. But chances were his older twin would see him and come along, and that wasn't what Sterling wanted.

Actually, he felt like he hadn't been sure of what he wanted ever since Samuel ditched the family to stay at their aunt and uncle's ranch with his new lady friend. He hadn't known that they could just *do* that. Decide their own fates and just... do it, no matter the cost.

It was like a whole new world of options had been presented to him and he was too... scared to look at any of them? No, he wasn't *scared*. He was...

He didn't know what it was that made him not want to think about it, but pumping iron and getting his heart rate up helped him at least forget that for a while. Adrenaline started pumping, chasing away the uncertainty, making him assured and confident as he liked to be.

It was a good while later when he finally finished, wiping sweat down with one of the soft towels they always kept in the workout room, then tossing it in the hamper for their laundry service to take care of. They came about once a week, and along with their small staff of household workers, kept the overly large estate from falling behind.

...huh. Sterling had never thought of their house as oversized, but with Samuel gone, their youngest brother at college, and Solomon spending so much time in the city, there was a certain sort of emptiness to it he had never noticed before.

He tried his best to dismiss that idea as he made it back to his room then showered. That made him feel a bit better, scrubbing the dirt from the ranch off along with his sweat. A small escape, but one he dragged out for probably longer than his skin would have liked.

Oh well.

Eventually, however, his fingers were pruning a little *too* insistently, so he forced himself out. From there, he grabbed more towels for the laundry service to clean and dried off, getting dressed in his comfortable nightclothes. He sat back down at his desktop—one that he'd gotten during his college years to play video games and work on projects with but mostly sat unused lately—when he noticed an email notification sitting in the corner of his screen.

Clicking on it, he was surprised to see that Elizabeth had lived up to her word, and the report was sitting right there waiting for him. He wasn't sure *why* he was surprised, considering how gung-ho she was already, but maybe he was just used to a certain sort of detachment from the business side of the ranch.

Sterling opened it, not quite sure what to expect. But it certainly wasn't anywhere near the *five-page* list of what she thought needed improvement.

But the real kicker was, it wasn't just an endless list demanding money for fixes. There was a reason why as well as hyperlinks to either a website where such things could be bought online or companies that provided the recommended services. She even wrote reviews under each link, with only a couple of them stating *could not find verified feedback, further research needed.*

If Sterling had tried to put together the same thing, it would have taken him *days.* Maybe even a week or two. But she'd come onto the ranch, thoroughly inspected the pens, and basically wrote a dissertation on what he and his family were doing wrong. In fact, they'd been doing so much wrong that apparently a whole team of specialists was needed. People and things he didn't have any access to without involving the business. So far, he'd just planned to use his personal expense account. But what she was recommending was basically in another league.

He could just fire her. Tell her that her goals were too lofty. Maybe even dismiss her as a bleeding heart who cared more about animals than people—that was his father's usual go-to. It would be the easiest solution, and Sterling sure did like easy solutions.

And yet, he didn't do that at all. Instead, he typed a measured response, at least in his opinion, stating that they needed to discuss it the next day. Once that was done, he realized that he'd spent much more time in the gym and the shower than he'd expected to, a little over three hours, and he was so utterly *exhausted* all of a sudden.

Shutting his computer down, he headed to the king-sized bed in his bedroom attached to his lounge and slid under the covers. But even as he laid there, letting his body relax, sleep wouldn't come to him.

...what exactly had he gotten himself into?

8

Elizabeth

*E*lizabeth couldn't lie to herself; she had been nervous sending out her full report, something that was rare for her. But what she was asking for was a lot, *a lot-a lot*, and there was the voice in the back of her head that said they were just going to kick her out and tell her the pigs were fine as they were.

But it was only because the pigs were so very *not* fine that she hit that send button, and at least Sterling didn't fire her outright on reply.

He didn't exactly agree either. So, she headed to work, expecting the worst but hoping that maybe, just maybe, something good might happen. But when she saw his truck already at the barn, his long, well-built figure leaned up against the side of it like something out of a movie, her gut churned with anxiety.

It would be a bummer to lose the job after one day, even if part of her still believed that it was too good to be true. But still, even a day of pay would help her a *long* way while she hunted around for a new job, and she got the feeling from Teddy that Silas would never allow for her to get ripped off for her time.

"Morning," she said as she stepped out of her car, squaring her shoulders and putting her best business face on. "You're up early."

"I'm always up early," he answered steadily, pushing himself off his truck to stand upright.

"Really? You don't seem like the up and at 'em type."

He smiled crookedly at that, tipping his head just slightly so that his hat cast a slight shadow over his face. "Used to not be, but then Silas took to riding at the crack of dawn, and I guess me and him just got into the habit of chasing the sun."

The thought of him and his brother both riding across the flats of the ranch, hair whipped back in the wind, drenched in the honey-gold of the morning flashed across Elizabeth's mind, and that was certainly a pretty sight. But she pushed that aside when the logical part of her brain caught up with his words.

"I haven't seen any horses around here."

"They're mostly on the opposite side of the pens. More towards the cows and the fields. These guys are a recent thing my family started and wasn't sure they wanted to pursue."

Ah, that explained why everything was so slapdash. "Perhaps that was something that should have been thought about a little more beforehand, given what I've observed."

"Yeah, you observed a whole lot, didn't you?"

Well that was a sentence that gave away absolutely nothing. "It's what you're paying me for, isn't it?" *And hopefully will continue paying me for.*

"I suppose so. And a lot more, it seems, going by your list."

"I wanted to be thorough."

"That much was obvious. Shall we go to the main house to discuss things? I have my office there as well as a computer."

A sliver of trepidation went through her. She was familiar with barns, with animals; that was her comfort spot. She definitely did not feel the same about McMansions owned by her employers. But he had a point. If they were going to go through her recommendations, having a computer and a desk would be prudent.

...would also be a really good place to fire her.

Withholding a sigh, Elizabeth nodded. "I guess I'll follow you in my car."

"Great." There was that crooked grin again. Surely, he wouldn't smile at her like that and then fire her... right? ...*right*? "I'll go slow."

She gave a nod and then they were off, either going to her inevitable doom or the world's most awkward house tour. Sterling didn't really go *slow* per se, but it certainly wasn't as quick as he had driven when he'd received the emergency call about Peggy, so at least there was that.

But all thoughts about speed fled from Elizabeth's mind as the mansion came into view. No, mansion wasn't even the right word for it. It was practically a *castle*.

The thing was *huge*. Sprawling. Basically, a town in its own right. Sure, yeah, maybe the large center part was a mansion, three stories tall at least with balconies on the top floor and several bay windows. But there were six wings that split off in different directions, almost like a star or flower. It was bigger than any mall Elizabeth had ever seen and about four times as fancy.

She pulled up behind Sterling at what she assumed was a side door, considering the nice garage that could probably house about two families in it, just sitting a bit away, and before she could think it through, words were tumbling out of her mouth.

"I don't understand how you can put all of this money into a place you couldn't possibly fill up while your animals don't have proper care."

Well... that wasn't very diplomatic. But their giant mansion spoke of money, and if they had *that* kind of money, then all of their animals should have the latest and greatest in husbandry. Was it just the pigs that were shorted? What if the rest of their livestock were in similarly awful conditions? What kind of excuse did they have?

"You're here to help that, aren't you?" he said, leading her inside.

They went an impossible route, down a hall, up a flight of stairs, down another hall; she wouldn't have been able to find her way back if she tried. But eventually they ended up in a small, office-like room complete with a desk, a couple of chairs in front of it as well as behind it, and several bookcases. It wasn't exactly Sterling's style, or at least what she thought his style was, but it was certainly functional.

Sterling sat down behind the desk, pulling out some papers from a drawer and setting them in front of her, then pulling out a red pen.

"I'm not really an organizational type, so forgive me if this goes a bit slowly."

She leaned over to see that he had printed out her list, well... that was a good sign, right? "A man of the earth or something?"

And then there was that smile again. Elizabeth thought that maybe God should put a limit on how much Sterling could use that grin.

His smooth voice continued, "I guess you could say that, at least recently." Before she could ask what he meant by that, he was turning the papers around so she could read it. "I'm telling you right now that we can't do all of these, so you and I are going through this one by one until we decide on what's absolutely necessary during a first pass, and what can be added later once we've proved that this is a worthwhile investment."

"The care of animals is always a worthwhile investment."

He paused a moment, his pen hovering over the paper, and his head tilted to the side as he regarded her. "Yes, you would think that."

"Because it's the right thing to think."

He didn't say anything regarding her last statement and instead pointed to the first item. "Now, I noticed you started with the no or low-cost improvements, but I was wondering how burying some logs and putting chains through some of them will help the pigs?"

Huh, he wasn't arguing with her. She supposed that was as good as any place to start. One by one, they went through the list. Most of the time he didn't make her parrot her whole explanation as to why they were needed—since she'd written most of them down in her report. Instead, he would ask her to clarify things he didn't understand or wanted to understand more completely. It was a negotiation, that much was clear, and Elizabeth found herself enjoying the challenge.

"And what's this? A heat lamp? I wasn't aware our pigs were freezing, considering it's the middle of summer."

"You'll note that I said it was for the indoor area and the birthing pens, as it's good for piglets. I figured it would be prudent to make you aware of the need for them ahead of time instead of waiting until its cold enough to be an issue."

"Smart. You always think so far ahead?" If it were anyone

else, she might have thought that was an insult, but his eyes had that sort of mischievous spark to them, and she could tell that he was messing with her.

"What?" she answered smoothly. "Don't you?"

"Fair enough. So, heat lamps it is."

Back and forth, back and forth, over and over again, banter flowing like a tennis match. She didn't win on everything. A few of the things were put on a list for "later," and a few were just dismissed as not an option at the moment. Strangely enough, she enjoyed the challenge, feeling like her brain was more active then than it had been in ages at the vet's office. She loved it.

By the end of the list, they'd come to an agreement on every item, and Elizabeth was utterly exhausted. She hadn't even done that much, and a quick look to her phone revealed that it was just barely lunchtime.

"How has it only been three and a half hours?" she asked with what she hoped was a wry smile. "It feels like we've been discussing terms of surrender for a decade."

"Terms of surrender?" Sterling asked with a chuckle. "That's one way to put it."

She shrugged. "Seemed appropriate considering how much the price tag for this is."

"That's fair enough. Well, since I'm already hemorrhaging money, how about we go grab some lunch? I could use some, that's for sure."

Elizabeth wasn't sure about that, the corners of her lips pulling down into a frown. "I'm not sure—"

"Come on, what better terms for peace than a meal to smooth things over? Besides, I don't know about you, but I'm tired of the sound of my own voice. Stuffing my mouth with food so I don't have to talk sounds like a much better idea."

He had a point. And she didn't want the feeling with her to fade, so she found herself nodding her head. "Sure. Why not?"

"Great. We'll take my truck. Might as well save gas."

Elizabeth didn't say it, but she doubted that Sterling or anyone in his family ever had to worry about saving gas ever in their entire lives. "Alright."

They headed back out the impossible maze made of riches that surely no one really needed and then outside down to his truck. She hopped in, wondering if she was crossing some sort of professional boundary, but her rumbling stomach and good mood encouraged her to take the risk.

He took off, driving more the speed that she was used to from their first meeting, and she thought that perhaps he was taking her to the worker lunch building. But they flew right by the dirt path that led to that, and she recognized the road that led out to the main road.

"Uh, where are we going?" Elizabeth heard herself ask tightly. She probably wouldn't have agreed if she had known that they were going to be leaving the premises. Her purse, her ID, everything was in her car, and she didn't like being separated from it.

But Sterling seemed surprised by her reaction, giving her an odd look. "We're getting food. My favorite grill place is in the city. Is that an issue?"

"It could be." She took a deep breath. She didn't need to lose her temper, even if she was being whisked off from her work. "Look, a person's time is valuable to them, and if you're planning on doing something that's going to consume more than three hours, then you should communicate that and get permission. As a courtesy."

He didn't say anything for a long moment, his gaze

returning to the road. They exited the *very* long driveway and turned onto the main road, not even the radio playing.

"Sorry," he said finally, although it sounded like the words caused him physical pain. Like they had to fight their way out of his mouth and into the air. "I didn't realize."

"Thank you. I appreciate that."

He nodded, turning up the radio. In the back of her mind, Elizabeth couldn't help but think that she was lucky that he was so spoiled and *just* bordering on inconsiderate. It was one thing to *look* like Prince Charming, it would be another thing entirely if he acted like it too.

9

Sterling

*I*t was a quiet ride into the city and Sterling felt like he *should* say something, but for the life of him couldn't figure out what had happened. He'd asked Elizabeth to lunch, she'd agreed, and then apparently, he'd been in the wrong for assuming that she would be alright with going into the city.

But... where else would they go *out* to eat? If he just wanted any food or to cook for himself, he would have just said they were going to the kitchen. When Elizabeth explained that he needed to ask, it had made sense, but it had also seemed... really weird. His first instinct had been to tell her that she was being pedantic, or needlessly picky, but something kept his mouth shut.

That wasn't something that happened often.

"So, this is your favorite place, huh?" Elizabeth asked as he parked. For some reason, he'd decided to park instead of using the valet service, leaving them both to walk across the parking lot of the restaurant.

"Yeah, why?"

"Well, I'm not sure if I expected something much fancier, or something more hole-in-the-wall."

"Nah, I'm not into all of those high-end bistros that serve you two drops of food and call it a meal. A man needs his protein, you know."

"Sure, because you're a growing boy."

"That *is* what my mom says," he quipped right back. He liked that she could keep up with him, that his money didn't seem to have any sort of sway over how she treated him. She challenged his mind and his wit, and sometimes the way she looked at him made him... made him...

Want to be better.

Truly, a ridiculous thing to think, especially since she was an employee that he had just met, and yet he was quickly realizing that that was how he felt anyway. There was disappointment in her gaze every time she looked around at the pigs, or at his family's wealth, which was pretty much the opposite of what he was used to. Her eyes didn't go wide, she didn't suddenly start fawning all over him. Yeah, she still very obviously wanted his money, but not for herself. After going over that list dozens of times and re-examining everything, there wasn't any way she was getting a drop of the money. She just really cared about the animals.

"I've never been here," she remarked as he held the door open for her, her dark eyes looking around. Her expression gave away nothing, but he liked that too. She was something to puzzle out. Most people were so easy to read, but the veterinarian in front of him? Not so much.

"I haven't been coming to the city much the past month or so because of a project I'm working on, but I used to hit this place up at least once a week." He waved to the host who straightened and headed around the almost desk-like station.

"Mr. Sterling," he said pleasantly. "Your usual seat?"

"Thanks, Max."

He didn't miss how Elizabeth's eyes went up to her hairline, which was meticulously kept. He couldn't be sure, but he was pretty certain she had what was called "natural hair" that she kept pulled back into a bun for the most part. He wondered what it would look like if she did any of the intricate braids he occasionally saw or brushed it out into a fully realized afro. She'd probably look too much like a Hollywood star or model, and he imagined ignorant people would take her even less seriously.

A shame, really. Even if he wasn't sure what to think of the woman, it was clear that she was relentlessly, painfully confident, and nothing would ever truly get in her way. She was kind of like watching a tornado go by. Beautiful, but a force of nature, and best to stay out of its path.

"You weren't kidding, were you?" she asked as the host led them over to a corner table near the back.

"It sounds impressive, but my usual isn't one specific place. Rather a set of requests. I like a two-to-four-top table with a clear line of sight to both the door and the bar, but away from the restrooms."

"That's... particular." Again, her tone betrayed nothing as they sat, the hostess setting down the menus. There was a pause as she said their server's name and that they would be with them in just a moment, but then the conversation slid right back into place like it was never interrupted.

"Really? You've never had to make a quick getaway when seeing someone unpleasant coming in where you're eating?"

"No, but then again, I've never dated two people at the same time."

Sterling felt his stomach drop, and his gaze flicked up to her face quickly. But her expression wasn't judging, or even all that sly. Like everything else, it was matter of fact and forthright. "How'd you hear about that?"

"You know, word gets around. Especially when the upstanding son of a mega-rich family is juggling a few other rich girls at the same time."

Sterling sighed. "It wasn't like that, you know."

"It wasn't? Then how was it?"

"Madison wanted to go on and get her Masters, but her parents told her she would lose too much valuable time when the goal was getting married and having children. At the time, with Solomon wrapped up in a possible engagement that hadn't fallen through yet, I was the next best choice to make a strategic alliance with."

"Not Silas? Or your oldest brother?"

Sterling scoffed. "Samuel? Dad would toss himself off a cliff before including him in anything important about the business. As for Silas, he's too useful. My dad needed someone who he could potentially lose a chunk of his access to and not hurt the day-to-day function of our enterprise. Enter me.

"I was all set to tank it, you know, no one likes being the spare wheel. Or a bargaining chip. But that Madison, she's a keen one. She could tell I wasn't really interested, at least not in the way I was supposed to be."

"And what way is that?"

Sterling shrugged. He didn't know why he was spilling his guts to a stranger, exposing the messy parts of his private life, but he didn't want her to think he was someone who juggled multiple women just for fun.

"You know, all roving hands and pressuring someone to go farther than they want. Don't get me wrong, I like flirting. I like banter. I even like looking at very pretty people. But I'm never going to be *that* type of guy. I don't want sex for the sake of sex, or pleasure for just the sake of pleasure. All seems a bit hollow, you know?"

"That's not a bad thing, you know that, right?"

That wasn't quite the response he expected. He thought she might say something was wrong with him or ask if he'd been traumatized as a kid. Unsure what to say, he just shrugged. "Depends on who you ask."

Her full lips pressed tightly together, as if she wanted to say something in particular, but in the end, she just sighed and moved on. Curious.

"So, this Madison could tell all that?" she asked.

"Well, maybe not all of it, but enough to find me in private and ask if we could go through the motions long enough for her to sign up for grad school and get started, all under the guise of me wanting to make sure anyone I married was an 'appropriately educated candidate.'" He couldn't help a wry smirk at that. "Which is hilarious considering I only barely have my bachelor's. But anyway. It worked. She started school, her parents laid off of her and set her up all pretty, and we pretended to date."

"So, where did the others come in?"

"Like I said, Madison was smart. And desperate. I don't think there's anyone quite as wily as a desperate, intelligent woman, and apparently that gene ran in her family because she and her sister approached me together about three months in.

"You see, Valerie was a lot like Maddy, except she didn't want to go to school. She just wanted to travel, see the world. Her father was eyeing some oil tycoon's son to set her up with, and I got the feeling she was about as interested in any romance about the same as you might be interested in a stubbed toe."

"I don't get it. Arranged marriages aren't a thing in this day and age, right? But you're really making it seem like a thing."

Sterling blinked at her for a split second. *Arranged what?* "I... I wouldn't use those words. All of us can say *no* at any time. Solomon did, in fact. It's just that you have to weigh if that 'no' is worth the consequences."

There was another break as the server approached them, asking them what they wanted to order. Sterling realized he hadn't even looked at the menu and neither had Elizabeth, so he laughed and asked for a few more minutes.

He had every intention of picking up his menu as soon as the waiter was gone and choosing something, but then Elizabeth was speaking again, and his whole world narrowed down to her.

Just her.

"*Consequences?*" Her voice was steady, but there was a strain to it. Like she was forcing the neutrality into her tone. "Like... punishment? Did—were... none of you were *hit* or something, were you?"

Another laugh. He really didn't mean to, but the idea of his older, shorter father trying to lay into Solomon was an amusing thought. But when he thought of Maddie and Val, the image was much more sobering. Alright, maybe a laugh wasn't the most appropriate reaction.

"No. Nothing like that. At least not as far as I know. But there are other things that can be used for leverage. Positions in the company. Trust funds. Inheritance. For Madison, I knew her father could reach out to his friends and get her attendance blocked from the school she wanted to go to. He could freeze her bank accounts, even though they were in her own name.

"Sure, she told me that she had been saving up and hiding money away ever since she turned fourteen, but even then, she couldn't trust that her parents wouldn't try one of their connections to keep putting pressure on her until she dropped out.

"Even Solomon, who basically was the golden child of our family for five years, got a temporary hell rained down on him. Father sent him to deal with the most taxing clients, doubled his workload, fired his assistants, yelled at him all the time. Honestly, I thought my brother was beaten until Frenchie came along and apparently gave him a spine again."

"Frenchie?"

Sterling waved his hand. "Long story, maybe another time. Point being, no, they're not arranged marriages, just negotiations. All of us have to walk the fine line of being our own people and keeping our parents happy."

"And the three of you figured you fake-dating both of them would be walking that line?"

"Well yeah. You see, what our parents hate the most is any sort of deliberate rebellion. Telling them no. Cause, ya know, even though we're adults, we're not allowed to say *no.*

"But if it turns out that a big alliance falls through because their son is just a cad of a young man, doing what any 'red-blooded young man would do given the temptation.'" He used air quotes for that one, just to make sure Elizabeth knew what he thought of *that* particular line of thinking. "That's much more acceptable. Sure, I got in plenty of trouble, but it lasted about a week as opposed to Solomon's *months,* and I've pretty much eliminated myself from any future consideration. Maddie is almost done with her degree now, having to 'take a break from romance to heal her broken heart,' and as far as I know, Val is still abroad, discovering about herself after I nearly 'turned her against her own sister.' It really worked out even better than we could have planned."

Elizabeth shook her head, letting out an incredulous sort of breath. "You know how crazy this all sounds, right?"

Sterling shrugged. "It's a different world, I guess. I'm sure there are things about your life that would seem insane to me."

Her somewhat disbelieving expression shifted into a wry sort of grin. "Oh, of that I am absolutely certain. But speaking of insanity, can you explain to me how any sort of burger is worth twenty-five dollars?"

Sterling found himself staring at her again, trying to figure out if she was being funny in that dry, sarcastic way of hers. But her expression stayed steady.

"Is that bad?" he asked. "You're kidding, right?"

She had to be joking. He liked the grill because it was cheap and fast. He and his brothers could eat out for usually around a hundred or so, maybe two hundred if all seven of them went. But that hadn't happened since they were teenagers and preteens. In fact, he didn't think he'd ever gone to a restaurant with his whole entire family in over a decade.

"Aren't you?"

More staring and it was getting to be downright awkward. Clearing his throat, Sterling looked from his menu to her. "What would be a normal burger price?"

"For every day? Never more than five bucks. If I'm treating myself out, twelve dollars, but that's pushing it."

It was his turn for his eyes to go wide. "*Twelve bucks* is a treat?"

He spent more than that on coffee when he went to the city. And he didn't even really *like* coffee.

"Look, going out at all is a treat for most people, and something I haven't been able to do since I graduated. I've got to save up to get a new car, since you've seen firsthand how mine is falling apart. Which, you know, is hard to do now on top of student loans."

Ah, Sterling understood that. Of course, his parents had paid for his school, but he had plenty of acquaintances in his major who'd had to take out exorbitant loans that they'd be paying on until the day they died.

He didn't understand that, of course, considering the Bible itself said that loans with interest were a sin, but he never really took the time to think about it.

"How much do you owe?" he asked before he could think better of it.

"About ten thousand. I was really lucky and landed a lot of the scholarships that I applied to. *A lot*. It was practically a job, really. Although it'll be more like thirty thousand when I actually pay all of it off, due to those predatory interest rates."

If he was like his father, Sterling would have told her that she could have just *not* taken them. But how else was she supposed to become a veterinarian? If she wanted a good job, she had to invest, and if her family didn't have enough to invest, then what else could she do besides get loans?

"Only 10K?" he asked with a laugh. "Why draw it out then? Just pay it off."

And she was staring at him again with that *look*. "Just pay it off?"

"Yeah. I know drawing things out can raise your credit, but if it's gonna cost you three times as much, just pay it off."

"Just pay it off," she repeated for the second time.

"I mean, you're a vet, right? Why are you saying it like that? I saw the average salary, that would be easy for you to pay off in a year and still buy a new car."

She choked on her water, setting the glass on the table with a *thunk*. "Just pay it off. Just pay it off, he says," she rasped around her coughing. "People don't just 'pay off' loans like that willy-nilly."

"I... I'm not understanding."

"Look, I *just* graduated, and it took me about seven months to even get a job, and I certainly didn't have the best pay rate working as a secondary vet at a family clinic in the city. A clinic I was *fired* from, by the way.

"I'm still paying off my mother's funeral, trying to help my father whose retirement is barely enough to cover his bills, and then pay all of my own bills.

"So not only is it not *easy* to 'just pay it off,' it's not practical. It wouldn't be practical for most people."

That didn't seem right. Her father's retirement couldn't pay his rent? Where was he living? And she'd been fired? No wonder her face had grown pale when he'd offered her a salary in the 80K range.

But still, it was only ten thousand dollars. He'd spent double that on a short vacation. He couldn't imagine that kind of money being out of grasp. It didn't make sense.

"Fine, I'll just pay it off here and now, if it's such a big thing," he said.

She froze, her eyes going wider than he had ever seen, and they had gone plenty wide already in the conversation. "What?"

"Maybe it's not practical for you, but it's nothing for me. So, I'll just pay it off for you."

"That's not a nice thing to joke about."

He didn't like that look across her face. One that was a mix of surprise, distrust and hurt. That wasn't how she was supposed to react. If he was doing something she couldn't, she should be happy, right? It wasn't like it was inconveniencing her. His expense account got about twenty thousand added to it every month, and most of the time it sat there, barely used. And that wasn't counting his *personal* salary or the money from the investment portfolio Silas had built for him.

"I'm not joking. I'm serious. If it's a trouble for you, let me do it. I promise you; I won't even notice the money's gone."

He supposed he couldn't blame her for being skeptical. His father would have an apoplexy if he knew his middle son was giving money away. But surely *that* had to convince her that he was genuine.

Her expression slowly slackened, and she picked up her glass of water, taking a long drink. Sterling could feel it; it was the moment he was going to sweep in just like Silas had with Teddy and save the day. Then *he* would be the good guy, the hero, and maybe people would recognize that he was worth something too.

"I..." she said slowly, as if she was thinking very hard on what to say next. But that next word never came. She sat there, blinking slowly, before suddenly standing and walking out.

...what?

Sterling was up and after her, laying a handful of bills on the table for the trouble. He caught up with her outside, walking purposefully towards the parking lot.

"Hey, Elizabeth! What's going on? Would you please *stop*?"

To his great surprise, she did, turning to face him. "You just don't *get* it, do you?"

Sterling pulled up short in front of her, feeling like he had failed some sort of test. "Get what?"

"Why I could possibly be upset."

He looked around, over her head, at their feet, trying to find his usual smooth, charming self. But that guy was gone, leaving him fumbling for an answer.

"No. I don't get it."

She took a deep breath. "Okay. Let me explain. I know you probably meant well, or at least didn't mean to harm me, but how you said things... set me off, I guess. First of all, I was jealous. Things are so *easy* for you. Easy enough that you wouldn't even miss ten *thousand* dollars. Meanwhile, I won't buy anything brand name at the grocery store, hoping that somehow all the cents will add up to fill my gas tank.

"I was embarrassed. I'm a grown woman, and I've fought so hard to end up where I am. But I'm struggling and barely getting by, and you have so *much.* It's hard not to feel embarrassed. It's also hard not to feel patronized. I worry day and night about those loans. I worry every single hour about money. And yet you're here saying you'd pay it off just because. Something that could destroy me wouldn't even make you blink.

"It's just so *unfair.* I work hard. My father works so hard. My mother died while working two jobs. But there you are, and here I am, just because you had the luck of being born into a rich family and I didn't."

Sterling didn't know what to say to that, his mouth going a bit dry. Sure, he knew there were poor people, folks who struggled, but he'd always thought that those who were truly impoverished were there due to bad decisions. But Elizabeth was making it seem otherwise.

So, what did that mean?

"I'm not sure what you want me to say."

"I don't think there is anything to say," she answered after another couple of beats. "It is what it is. It's not like you asked to be born into your family, either. Let's just let it go and... take me back to work."

Sterling swallowed, feeling like there was a lump of lead down in his stomach. Going through the expenses for the pigs had gone so well, how had it all fallen apart? They hadn't even eaten yet and she was asking him to drive her the hour and a half or so back to their estate. What kind of awkward ride would *that* be?

"Yeah. I can do that."

"Thanks."

10

Sterling

*I*t'd been a month since that not-a-lunch in the city, and Elizabeth had kept her distance ever since. If he came into a room, she usually left it. And if she didn't, it was because she was so embroiled in her work that she didn't notice him much.

The pigpen was still being worked on, of course, and then add on top of that the fact that Sterling was busy dodging his father, and that made for a pretty hectic day. Because of course McLintoc Miller had noticed all the expenses his middle son had incurred in the past month, and of *course* he was on the warpath for it.

But Sterling did have two particular advantages. One being that his father regularly forgot to wear his glasses, as if his subconscious physically rejected the idea that he was getting old and needed them. The second was that he was an identical twin. And that second advantage had never been so apparent as when his father had managed to corner him in the kitchen, all red-faced and looking right ornery.

Sterling had been so sure that was the end, that his dad was going to cut him off and maybe even send him to his aunt and uncle's place where his brother Samuel was. But instead, his father had called him Silas and demanded to know "what in tarnation his younger brother was doing." Naturally, Sterling hadn't bothered to correct his father on the error, but he sure didn't like the feelings it had stirred up in him.

"Is that really how I looked when I was pining over Teddy?" Silas said, pulling Sterling's mind away from his thoughts.

"I'm not *pining*," Sterling grumbled, perhaps more crankily than he should have given the situation. He was on top of one of their silos, helping his twin repair a part that the wind had taken off in a spring storm a month or so back. "I just know that I messed up, but don't really get how, or how to fix it. And it feels like I *should* fix it so that there's not bad blood on the ranch."

Silas let out a small chuckle. It was one that Sterling knew all too well that meant he thought his little brother was being particular. In other words: ridiculous.

"What's so funny?"

"There was plenty of bad blood when Dad tried to switch the insurance policies after Solomon put the kibosh on it, and we all made it through. So, if you're really worried about that, you don't need to be. As angry as Dad can get sometimes, he's running out of steam. And he knows that he has to walk the fine line of keeping us loyal to him while also being a complete dictator about things."

Surprise tugged at Sterling, making him forget about Elizabeth for a moment. "Is that what happened? That's what that whole fight was about?"

He vaguely remembered it happening before Teddy rolled around but after Solomon started spending a lot of time in the city. It was Sal who had spilled the beans about Frenchie, but the real tear up between their father and Solomon hadn't happened until at least a couple of weeks after that.

Any details post-fight were lost on Sterling, however, as he'd chosen to take a couple week vacation to Australia rather than stick around for all the tension. It was already bad enough after Samuel bailing.

"Yup. 'Fraid so. Thought he was going to write Solomon out of the will right then and there for daring to say no to him, but somehow he survived." Silas wrinkled his nose. "Although, to be honest, it hasn't gotten much better. I wouldn't be surprised if he pulled a Samuel any day now and took off with whatever money he's got squirreled away."

"I don't know what to say to that." That seemed to be happening more and more lately, and Sterling didn't like it. He may have not been the smarter twin, or more useful twin, but he was always the smoother twin. The charmer. The *flirt*. If that got taken away, did he have anything besides his money?

That was a hollow life if he ever heard of one.

But... when he thought about it... did he really have much else? Sure, he had plans with his soil tests and now the pigpens, but what did he actually *contribute* to the world? Anything? He could spend money well. He'd helped a couple girls who were in a tough situation. But hadn't most of that been really about helping himself out? Would he even have done it if he hadn't been almost certain that it would get him out of any future engagement shenanigans for at least a while?

"Yeah, I'm not too keen on it either, if I'm being honest,"

Silas said, reaching out for Sterling to hand him the tinsnips. He didn't need to verbalize what he was asking for; they were long past that. Had been since they were ten. "And the more time I spend with Teddy and the community center, the more I can see why our brothers feel the way they feel."

Sterling wanted to tell his twin not to be dramatic. That their family did plenty for the community, like helping fund the restoration of that one church after a bad storm. Or contributing to political campaigns that needed support. But no matter how he turned what Silas said this way and that in his head, it didn't seem like something good people would do.

And if his family weren't good people, if *he* wasn't a good person, what all did that mean?

If that was the kind of doubt that came along from trying to be the hero in someone else's story like Silas, well then, he changed his mind. He didn't want any of it. It was far too exhausting and left him feeling like he didn't have any solid ground to stand on.

Sterling had never been much of a fan of falling.

11

Elizabeth

She really shouldn't be outside.

Elizabeth knew that much. In fact, a not-so-small voice was practically screaming it from the back of her head, and yet she hadn't listened.

Classic Elizabeth.

She hadn't meant to put herself in such a position. One moment she'd been working, the next a sudden storm swept in right before the end of her shift.

She should have gone into the main house for protection. Should have left. The garage and the worker's shop were both too dangerous, considering the intense winds and how many sharp implements hung out in both those places. The smart thing to do was to get shelter and be safe.

...but she wasn't doing that at all.

Ignoring the near frenzied voice telling her to find cover,

she stood a few feet away from the pens, finishing up the very last-minute checkups of work done for the day. She wanted to make sure that no one cut corners. Even if she trusted Sterling —which she didn't—that didn't stop the contractors they'd brought in from trying to pull one over on the both of them.

It was getting to be almost impossible to see with the rain starting to slant sideways, driven like bullets in the malevolent gusts. Although the work tablet she had been given was incredibly fancy and "water-resistant," she couldn't help but wonder if she was pressing that to its limits.

Finally, the voice screaming in the back of her head won out, and she decided to stop being reckless. It was just so hard for her to leave something undone, grating at her nerves like a half-finished homework sheet or project.

Oh well. Better safe than sorry, something her mother had always tried to teach her.

Tucking her tablet under her arm and her stylus in her already soaked hair—which was going to be *awful* to deal with once she was home—she sprinted to her car.

Well... she *tried* to sprint. Against the wind and the rain, it was more of an unsteady lope. But whatever one called it, she made it to her vehicle and threw open her door to practically throw herself in. Her hands shook with a bit of a chill, the wind negating the normal summer warmth. Blearily, she only barely got her car started when she heard an awful, ear-piercing sort of sound.

It was distorted, carried over to her on the wind and twisting in on itself, coiled like a specter's last haunting cry. But then it sounded again, a terrible, *terrible* yowl.

Something was hurt.

She was back out of the door before she could think about it, looking for the source of the sound. It was a small creature;

she was almost certain. If she had to put money on it, could be a feline. Maybe a fox or coyote. Definitely *very* scared.

It sounded again, almost floating to her through the increasingly violent storm. A desperate SOS, a plea that didn't expect to get answered. She took off in the direction of the noise, one hand holding her ruined hair out of her eyes.

It was so impossible to see. It was like the world had been dipped in gray paint and was trying to violently shake it off. The wind was growing sharper and meaner, its teeth biting into her like it wanted to yank off whole trunks as trophies. But she pressed on, following the desperate, horrid yowls.

And against all the odds, she spotted it. She didn't know how, but she did. There was a cat, stretched out, bristling and completely soaked a dozen or so feet away from her. It looked to be a calico, all patches of white, orange, brown and cream, and Elizabeth didn't need to see it clearly to know it was *very* upset.

As she sprinted over, sliding slightly in the mud, she realized that a heavy piece of equipment had fallen over and one of her front paws was stuck under it, trapped between that and another errant piece of shrapnel. Strange, sure, for something as dexterous as a cat, but not unheard of.

"Hey there, friend," Elizabeth said as soothingly as she could. Normally she would give a cat a chance to sniff her. Do some slow blinks to show she wasn't a threat in that way that cats liked. She would let the cat invite her into its space. But normally she wasn't rescuing a feline from errant machinery in the middle of a freak storm. "I'm going to approach you. I'm going to touch you in ways you probably won't like. I need you to stay calm for me, okay? Let's work together."

The cat meowed at her again, sorrowful and weaker by the moment. She didn't have time to waste. Going over to it, she saw how the equipment tipped. It was too heavy for her to pick up completely, but she could definitely rock it off the cat's paw. The poor thing would probably run off the moment it was free, but that was okay. At least it wouldn't be trapped.

In some sort of small miracle, she was able to move it just long enough for the cat to yank her paw back, but surprisingly, she didn't run. Instead, she inched forward tentatively, like she was terrified of the contraption but not willing to leave it.

"Hey, what's going on now? Are you—"

But then she heard it.

Barely audible over the howling wind. The tiniest, *teeniest* sliver of a mewl. And a cry. And then other mewls.

Kittens.

Elizabeth was on her knees in that same breath, not caring if mud soaked through the knees of her jeans. Whipping her phone out, she shook it to activate the flashlight and looked into a recess barely visible under the twisted metal.

And it was there, just behind some grating that might have been part of a door before but now most definitely was not, five little kittens. Their eyes weren't open, they were soaked, and they were voicing their displeasure with all the strength that tiny little kitten lungs had.

"Oh no, mama. I'm not gonna leave any of you out here."

She went from her knees to her belly, the mud happily clinging to her front pretty much instantly. The grating was tiny, but it was enough for her to slip her fingers through some of the gaps at the top and *tug*.

Once. Twice. Three times with all she had. The calico was trying to press up beside her arm, as if she was helping, but mostly she was just motivating Elizabeth further. She yanked again, hissing and letting out a long stream of curses as the metal grating sliced through one of her fingers. Her Pa wouldn't have approved of such language, but she could worry about that later.

Another yank. Another slice, this time through her palm. But she didn't stop. She could feel the grating giving way, bending, little by little until there was enough of a gap for her to shove her arm through and grab one of the kittens in the mud.

Thankfully it was still warm to the touch, and that allowed her to ignore the way the sharp metal bit into the skin of her arm, tore at the sleeves of her work shirt. None of that mattered. The only thing that was important was the little lives depending on her.

It was almost like she entered a trance. There wasn't any rain, weren't any tornado-force winds. It was just her, the mama and the kitties, all working together to make sure everyone was safe.

When the last one was over the barrier, she could have cried. But there was no time for that. Quickly, she sat back on her knees, shoving the kittens down into her shirt and then picking up the Mama and tucking her into the crook of her arm. Strangely, the cat didn't object, a small thread of a purr escaping her. It was comforting, especially since Elizabeth knew that a cat's purring could actually heal themselves and humans faster.

But even some good purr-therapy wouldn't do much if she stayed out in the maelstrom surrounding them. She needed to get them to shelter. She needed to get them *warm*, and while the mud was helping contain her body heat, all the wind and water wasn't.

She fought her way to her feet in the slick mud without the use of her hands, kittens wiggling in her shirt while mama just purred away. Trying to guess what direction her car was, she barely took a step before her entire world exploded with a bang.

Everything spun, violent and cruel, only for a deluge of pain to wash all of that away in a rush of blinding white. Elizabeth stumbled, barely able to catch herself on her knees.

Something had... hit her? Yeah, something had hit her. In the back of her head. She wanted to touch it, to see if the warmth there was just her body's response to the impact or if she was bleeding. But her hands were full, and she felt like if she tried to raise them above her head that she might keel over then and there, so she just pushed herself unsteadily back onto her feet again.

She had to find her car. She had to get to shelter.

It was like that song she used to listen to every Christmas as a kid. She just had to take one step. And then another. And then one more. Just a step, and then she would be at her car door. Or something like that.

She managed to get a good pace, going a bit further. She was almost certain she could see the outline of her car in the distance. It seemed almost impossible. Had she really run that far toward the cat?

She had to have... but that didn't seem right.

Her internal debate was interrupted violently when something *else* crashed into the back of her leg, heavy and far too dense. It was too much for her to stay steady, and she tripped again, her balance as scattered as the wind.

With the way she was falling, she knew she couldn't catch herself. At least not without her hands and possibly hurting the kittens. So she turned as best she could, landing square on her back and driving all of the air out of her lungs. It was amazing how much her body could register in slow motion. The initial blow on her shoulder blades and how it radiated outwards.

The lightning down her spine. Then her head hit the ground, bouncing off what felt like a rock peeking out of the wet muck. That was right when the world stopped making sense, both going fuzzy and spinning viciously at the same time.

Ow...

It was hard to think; in fact, her thoughts might have actually been soup. The only thing she could wrap any of her brain around was the cats. She had to get up. She had to help them. She was *so* close to her car.

But her body wouldn't cooperate. It was like someone had cut the strings that normally moved her limbs, and she was left lying there with no way to control her own form. She could feel the mud seeping into her clothes, stealing away her body heat. She could feel the wind scouring her. Heck, she could even feel the kittens squirming in her shirt. But none of that could help her figure out how to bend her legs or sit up.

And boy would it be nice if everything would stop *spinning*.

She was lost in that nonstop cycle of panic and confusion until, seemingly out of nowhere, strong hands were gripping her. She would have let out a shout if she had the wherewithal to do so, but she could only sputter blearily as she was pulled up. The hands were *warm*, so warm and nice against her skin, which felt like it had been scrubbed raw with a Brillo pad.

She wanted to say thank you; she wanted to explain why she was an idiot that ran out into the storm. But the only words that really came out were murmurs about cats, and Elizabeth let herself sink into that mantra. If the cats were safe, then everything would be okay.

12

Sterling

*H*e really shouldn't have been outside.

Sterling knew that much. He could practically hear Silas standing behind him, lecturing him how it wasn't safe and how he was going to get himself killed. And yet he was outside anyway, watching the insane storm that had rolled in like it needed vengeance and ASAP.

He wasn't just standing out in the drive for no reason, however. In a lot of ways, the storm outside seemed a lot like the one inside of him. He'd had a month and a half of feeling bad about how the lunch with Elizabeth had turned out, knowing he did something wrong but not entirely sure of what. He told himself that that day was the day, and he was going to confront Elizabeth and see if he could talk things out.

And then the storm started sweeping in.

It didn't look that bad, but he knew Texas well enough to be aware that a "not bad" storm could quickly become "a really bad" storm, and it wouldn't be wise to risk it. But it was the end of the day on Friday, and if he didn't talk to her in the next few minutes, he would have to wait until Monday to try again. And he knew from experience that she was always brusque and a bit cranky on Monday because she was catching up on anything she had missed with the contractors over the weekend.

Grumbling to himself, he headed to his truck and got in. He shouldn't even *have* to go talk to her, and yet he knew he had to. Or at least he did if he wanted to...

Wanted to what?

He left that question alone and focused on driving.

And it turned out that he certainly needed all of his focus because the storm *really* kicked in and it was almost impossible to see. He thought about turning around, because of course a capable woman like Elizabeth would know how to get herself out of danger. And yet he didn't. He just hunkered down, slowing his speed to make sure he didn't accidentally hit something.

He told himself he just wanted to check that she was heading home. Although she was smart, he knew she was an incredibly hard worker. Not out of any loyalty to his family, of course, but for the animals.

It definitely wasn't the safest driving, and the closer he got to the pens, the worse the storm grew. He couldn't see any other vehicles, so he was pretty sure that everyone had left, but what harm could there be in double-checking?

His answer came to him as he nearly hit something, slamming on his breaks when he noticed headlights right in front of him at the last second. He said some words his mother would not have been proud of, then threw his car into park.

The moment he opened his door, he was practically

slammed into the side of his truck. After a moment he caught his breath, but it seemed like hell itself had come to town for a visit. He could hardly see anything in the maelstrom around him, debris flying every which way and rain falling sideways, but he was pretty sure he'd been driving right down the middle of the car path. So, the biggest question was who had left their own vehicle smack dab in the center of the road, lights not even on bright?

He got his answer as he steadied himself and took a couple of steps forward. It was Elizabeth's car, it was running, her door was wide open and being practically ripped off its hinges by the storm, but she was nowhere in sight.

...what?

"Elizabeth!?" he called out into the storm, the wind snatching away his words the moment they left his mouth. "*Elizabeth!*"

No answer. For a moment he just stood there, dumbstruck and imagining about a thousand and one horrible things that could have happened to her, but then the tiniest of noise made it to him.

He tilted his head, trying to catch it better. It wasn't human, that was for sure, but whatever it had to be was quite piercing to make it all the way to him.

"Elizabeth!" he called again, heading towards where he thought that haunting, lingering sound might be coming from.

The going was *not* easy, with the wind buffeting him like it had a vendetta against him. Every time he lifted his foot, he felt as if he was going to be blown off his feet and taken to Oz. If the wind was affecting *him* that much, then what was it doing to Elizabeth? Sure, she was six feet tall and her frame was obviously very athletic, but he had at least fifty pounds on her.

The sound issued again, louder but more desperate. He had

no idea what it could be, and he was aware that he could be going towards an angry coyote or other small animal while Elizabeth was lost somewhere on the estate. But his gut told him that if there was an animal that was hurting, he could probably count on the veterinarian being there.

There was a *thunk* from somewhere in front of him, sounding loud and heavy, but he didn't pay it much mind until the toes of his boot collided with something hard. Jumping backward and opening his mouth to a spray of rain, he realized some of the metal roofing of their tool shack had been absolutely ripped apart, and a chunk of it was embedded into the ground right where he had been walking.

...that was not good.

That was most *definitely* not good.

Being out in a storm with the wind whipping around and visibility at zero was one thing, but razor-sharp and jagged pieces of metal were entirely another. He'd heard horror stories about such things decapitating people, or livestock. It was *not* what he or Elizabeth should be out in.

A voice in the back of his head, one that was oily and bright and slippery, whispered that he should just turn tail and go back to the safety of his truck. After all, Elizabeth was smart. She wouldn't be gallivanting around in such dangerous weather. He needed to make sure he was safe, then he could look for her once the coast cleared.

It was such an easy thought, and it would be nice to get out of the storm, to crank the heat in his truck on high and hunker down. And it would be a lie to say he wasn't tempted. His heart was thundering in his chest and every step felt like his last.

But he didn't listen. He kept on. Moving around the metal and bending forward to keep his center low. He raised one arm, curling it over his head to hopefully block any blows to his neck or skull. Not that his arm would stop a piece of metal sheeting flying at high speeds, but it was worth the effort.

"Elizabeth!" he called again, his voice seeming to go no further than a few feet in front of him before being gobbled up in the tempest. It was a greedy thing, hungry and wanting to snatch up everything it could. But it was wrong if it thought that it could beat him. Sterling may have been a lot of things, but he wasn't a coward.

...or at least he hoped not.

He pushed on, one foot in front of the other. He rounded a stack of hay bales, using his hand against them to guide himself. And he came out the other side just in time for something to crash to the ground in front of him.

"Elizabeth!"

For a moment he thought he was completely imagining it. But wiping the rain from his face showed that it was indeed Elizabeth who was lying on the ground in front of him, filthy and her shirt wriggling strangely.

His body was moving instantly, rushing to her side like there wasn't any rain, wasn't any wind. He didn't think anything coherent, or at least not as far as he could tell, his entire mind just blaring that he needed to help her. Help her *now*.

He gripped her under the shoulders, hauling her up. But as soon as he got her onto her feet, her knees started to buckle, so he swept his arm up under her legs until he had her in a bridal carry.

"It's the cats," she said, her eyelids fluttering at him.

"The what?"

"I had to. Cats."

"Right. The cats," he said. Clearly something was wrong, but he wasn't a doctor. He wasn't even medically inclined. Taking a deep breath, he marched back to his truck.

It wasn't easy. Although Elizabeth wasn't exactly heavy, she was solid and long-limbed, with her legs and arms catching in the wind. It was only when he was around the hay bales again that he realized they weren't quite alone.

There was a cat, drenched and covered in mud, tucked into Elizabeth's arm closest to his body. The thing looked up at him with doleful eyes, such a pitiful expression on its face that he kind of almost understood why Elizabeth was out there saving the little kitty.

That still didn't explain why the vet's shirt was wriggling slightly, but Sterling didn't have enough presence of mind to really worry about that. No, mostly he was worried about why Elizabeth seemed so out of it. Sure, the storm was awful, but that didn't really give an answer for her disorientation.

It was a fight back to his truck, but Elizabeth's extra weight helped ground him. By the time he got her there, his arms were aching, and his back was burning, but he threw his door open and got her inside.

She refused to let go of the cat, curling around it as he pushed her into the passenger side. Mud and water dripped down his seat and onto his floor, but he didn't care. The only thing that mattered was getting her safe and warm and maybe a little less dirty.

"I'm... the cats," she said again as he gently pushed her up to buckle her in. Sure, maybe he was wasting time, but considering the weather and visibility, he wasn't going to risk saving her just to accidentally kill her in some sort of vehicular freak accident.

It was then that his hand brushed against her front and he felt something very wet, warm and... squiggly? Cautiously, he put a slight bit more pressure on the spot only for it to mewl very quietly at him.

Did she...

Did she have *kittens* in her shirt!?

That certainly seemed to be the case, and he very carefully picked the mass up through her shirt and lifted it above the pressure of the seatbelt. Once he was sure they were all nestled safely, he shut the door and rushed to the driver's side, shaking his head.

How was it, of all the times and all the places, she found a mama cat and kittens in need? She seemed to have a sixth sense for animals in danger, and it was kind of amazing.

He just hoped that it didn't kill her.

No, that was far too morbid of a thought. Going faster than he should have, he raced back home. Part of him wanted to take her to the hospital, but he wasn't quite sure they'd make it there considering the storm. Besides, Mom had been training to be a nurse before she married Dad, so she would be of more help than ending up upside down in a ditch.

He had no idea how long it took him to get home. He didn't have much of a mind for anything else but driving and making sure that Elizabeth was still breathing. She looked an absolute *wreck,* and he'd never seen her so mussed, not even when helping a pig give birth.

Her hair tie must have snapped because her usual, no-nonsense bun was gone, revealing wild curls that were weighed heavy with rain and dirt. Her clothes were streaked in the filth and he couldn't be sure, but there seemed to be a red stain growing on the side of her leg.

Was she *bleeding!?*

His heart was in his throat as he pushed his truck as fast as he was willing, considering the conditions and the slight fact that he didn't want to kill her. But the last time he had been so terrified, so *truly* terrified had been when his brother Silas had grabbed that firework out of Sterling's hands—shouting about safety and losing fingers—only for it to go off right in front of the older twin.

At least Elizabeth didn't smell like burned flesh and hair. Sterling didn't think he would ever get that scent out of his mind. It had scoured his nose at the time, searing its way into his memory. He'd been so terrified then, and that same feeling was returning in full force.

Even though it wasn't his fault this time. Not like it'd been when they were kids.

Except it still felt like his fault. Elizabeth wouldn't have been out in the storm if he hadn't hired her. And yet, she wouldn't have a good-paying job or a chance to catch up on her bills without him hiring her. She'd made it quite apparent during their ill-fated lunch that she had a lot of financial troubles, and her previous job hadn't paid her as well as it should have.

Ugh, thinking about that meal did *not* make him feel any better, and he shut all of those thoughts out. He didn't have time for them. The only thing he had time for was to get her home and safe.

It seemed an age before he pulled right up to the side door, spraying the house with mud. Whatever. That could wait until later. Going back around to her side of the car, he pulled her out and carried her inside. She was muttering still, but it made even less sense than before.

He rushed to their main sitting room, which was down the short wing. He wasn't quite running, but he certainly wasn't walking either, and by the time he erupted into the room, he was covered in sweat.

"Mom!" he cried, seeing her sitting by one of the wide, bay

windows that held a reading nook. She had one of the books that Sal had gotten for her last Christmas, the last in a series.

"Sterling! What's—oh, the *mess!*"

"Never mind that," he said, rushing over to the thickest couch and setting Elizabeth on it. As soon as his hands were off her, she tried to sit up on her own, and Sterling gently tried to get her to lay still. "We got caught in the storm. She's hurt."

"Oh! Who is this?"

"This is a vet I have on contract.

NOW WILL you please call 911 and ask them what to do? It's too dangerous to take her all the way to the city."

"Right, of course. I'll just—" She shook her head and rushed over to the nook she had been sitting on, grabbing her phone. As Sterling knelt beside Elizabeth, he heard her dialing up 911. For him bursting in suddenly, she explained the situation quite well, and soon she was rattling off questions to her son. "Is she conscious?"

"Yeah," Sterling answered, looking at Elizabeth's face. "She's awake, but she doesn't seem to be very with it."

"They want you to ask her what day it is."

Sterling nodded, gently gripping Elizabeth's filthy hands in his. "Hey, do you know what day it is?"

"I..." She blinked at him, her eyes unfocused. "I... the kittens..."

"The kittens? What is she talking about?"

"She has them in her shirt, Mom."

"She *what?*"

"Not now! Elizabeth, do you know what day it is right now?"

"Uh? F-Friday. It's Friday. I was going to go home, but there were... there were kittens."

"Yes, I know. And you got them all."

"They said to ask her how old she is," Mom cut in, sounding quite worried.

He didn't blame her. He felt like he could hardly breathe.

"How old are you, Elizabeth?"

"That's... that's not a nice thing to ask a lady," she said with the weakest little laugh he'd ever heard.

"You're right. I suppose I've never been very good at being polite. Huh, Lizzy?"

There it was, that spark in her eyes that he was used to. "Don't call me Lizzy." That spark vanished as she groaned. "*Oh, my head hurts. It hurts so much.*"

"Mom, tell them that she's responsive now but still a little confused, and her head hurts a lot."

"I am standing right here, dear. I'm aware of what's happening in front of me."

"Right... Just tell them that, okay?"

She did, and they seemed to be having quite an exchange before she sighed and handed her phone to him. "They want to talk to you."

He took it, not removing his eyes from Elizabeth. "Hello?"

"Yes, sir, it sounds like your friend might have a concussion. Do you know if she lost consciousness at all?"

"I don't. I mean, when I found her she was awake but I don't know if she passed out for a second before I reached her."

"It would be best if you could get her here to see a doctor and have them examine her, but the weather is quite danger-ous. We can send one of our heavier duty ambulances—we have a few natural disaster rigs. It's on patrol right now, but it could take close to two hours to get to where your mother said you were."

"Two hours? That seems like a long time. Could waiting hurt her?"

"There is a chance that waiting could possibly exacerbate an injury. But there is also a chance that traveling in this weather could be gravely dangerous."

"It's fine. I'm bringing her in."

"But sir—"

He hung up, standing up. "Hey Elizabeth, are you alright to walk on your own?"

"Am I... am I what?"

"It's fine. Don't worry, I got you. Mom, can you get a box and some towels?"

"How will that help her?"

"It's for the cats, Mom."

"Right, of course. One moment."

She rushed off, and Sterling went about gently pulling Elizabeth's work shirt from where it was tucked into her pants since he certainly wasn't going the other way. One by one, he pulled the wiggly, very dirty kittens out, and finally the mama cat moved.

Sterling's mother was back a moment later with supplies for them. "Oh goodness, look at these poor things. Were they caught out in the storm?"

"That's definitely what I'm guessing."

"They were trapped," Elizabeth answered quickly before wincing, both of her hands going to the sides of her head. "I had to help."

"It's fine. I know you did," Sterling soothed, feeling a strange kind of emotion build in his chest. He wanted to soothe her, to comfort her. But mostly he wanted to go out and wrangle the storm itself for *daring* to hurt her. It was a bizarre sort of protectiveness that he'd never experienced before.

"I'll take care of these cats, dear. You help your vet friend," Sterling's mom said.

"You're not going to try to convince me not to go out in the storm?" Sterling asked.

The older woman sent him a wry sort of smile, the corners of her eyes crinkling in something that wasn't quite happiness. "Oh sweetie, I learned long ago there was no use in trying to convince any of you not to do something you've set your mind to."

"Fair enough. Hey, Elizabeth, I'm going to pick you up again. Just relax. I got you, okay?"

Her eyelids fluttered; the movement exaggerated by her long lashes. "Can I have some headache meds? My head hurts."

"Once we get to the hospital, okay?"

She said something else, but then he was picking her up and heading out. Thankfully she didn't flail or otherwise struggle, and soon they were right back into his mud-covered truck. Last-minute he ran back inside, grabbing several of the long, thick towels from the mudroom, then rushed back out. Swaddling Elizabeth and making sure her head was cushioned, he finally felt better speeding towards the main road.

Well, speeding was probably not the right word for it. Although it was easier to navigate closer to the estate, the world was still a dark gray with persistent rain going at practically a one-hundred-and-eighty-degree angle. It was the kind of storm that people would talk about for *months*, and it had come completely out of nowhere.

There was going to be so much damage, both in the city and across the countryside, but at the moment the only thing he really cared about was if the woman quietly groaning beside him was going to be okay.

13

Elizabeth

*F*uzzy.

Fuh-zzzey.

Everything was fuzzy.

Everything was fuzzy and blurry, and nothing made sense over the *blaring* horn of agony in her head. Ow. Ow. *Ow.* The same throbbing of hurt over and over again until she thought she might puke. Every time she thought she might almost have a thought, it rushed off in another vicious surge of pain. It was like someone had shoved two long fingers into her brain and was scrambling around her skull's insides just for funzies.

It was hell, that was the only word she had for it, and it felt like an age passed before the stabbing, throbbing, malicious pain softened just enough for her to breathe steadily. But it did start to ebb, ever so slightly, and after another age of just breathing in and out... in and out, her thoughts stopped being so fuzzy around the edges.

Where... where was she?

Blinking, Elizabeth opened her eyes to look around. Except they were already open, and it was like someone was sketching her surroundings in real time until she could finally *see* them as they actually were.

That was certainly trippy.

"Hello?" she called uncertainly before a wave of nausea had her hand going to her mouth. She managed not to upchuck, but it made the throbbing in her head return in full force for several seconds, and she had to work herself all the way back down again.

That was unpleasant, so she tried just moving her eyes around. As far as she could tell, she was in some sort of hospital-like setting. An ER, perhaps? The size of the room and the fact that it was curtained off seemed pretty indicative of an emergency room.

Almost as soon as she concluded as much, the curtain was opening and someone who she assumed was a nurse stepped in. "Hey there, you look more alert. How are you feeling?"

Elizabeth stared at her a moment, trying to remember anything of the past couple of hours. She remembered hands carrying her. A ride in the truck. She remembered a very strange phone call and then more riding. She also remembered that she went from being very, very cold and wet to being just damp and warm, a noted improvement.

Except... she was pretty sure that she was dry.

Looking down her body cautiously, she realized that she was in a hospital gown. That was strange. "Who changed me?" she heard herself ask, voice gravelly.

"You did, sweetie. I mean, I was there to make sure you didn't fall down, but you insisted on doing it yourself."

"I don't remember that."

"You don't? Okay then, love, do you mind telling me what you *do* remember?"

Elizabeth did so, and the nurse came up alongside the bed she was in. The woman didn't seem condescending, just appropriately concerned, and her smile was sweet once Elizabeth shakily finished.

The nurse nodded her head. "Alright, so it seems like you missed quite a bit there. I'm going to tell the doctor that, okay? You're currently in our ER, which I figured you guessed since you were so calm about me poppin' in here. As far as the doctor said, you don't need to be admitted overnight, but they did some tests and are waiting for a couple of results to come back.

"You've been conscious the whole time, and able to answer questions for the most part, but you have been very confused. Please don't be surprised if random memories of this time come back to you over the next week or so. You took a nasty hit to the head."

"Can I have a glass of water?" It felt like her mouth was filled with mud and grit. She hated it.

"Sure, let me go grab that for you. It's on your charts that it's fine for you to have clear liquids right now. I'll be right back." The nurse headed out but, true to her word, she came right back with a plastic cup. "Your friend is still out in the waiting room; we need your permission to disclose your status to him."

"My friend?"

"The man who brought you in. You know, he's over six feet tall, chiseled jawline. Real intense eyes, if you ask me."

"Oh. *Sterling.* Yeah, you can tell him he can come in. He's my boss."

"Wow, from what I heard he had quite the trip to bring you here. That's a pretty good boss."

She gave the woman a kind of shrug. "I suppose so." He wasn't a *bad* boss, per se, but there was some awkwardness with what had happened at their one lunch. And it was hard not to resent him a little for being just *so* filthy rich.

But then again... the hands that had picked her up... had they been his? Had he saved her? If that were true, what was he even doing out in the fields? He mostly avoided the pens ever since that trip to the city. And he certainly *never* was there at the end of the day.

"Hey there," Sterling said softly as he entered, looking sheepish. He also had a whole ton of mud on him, lending credence to her theory that he had indeed been the mysterious hands that had helped her. "You're looking better."

"I feel better," she answered honestly. "A lot more like myself."

He let out a sigh of relief that surprised her, and he shot her a soft smile. "You were definitely out of it. Very concerned about the cats."

That startled a memory back to her, and she sat up so quickly that her head spun. "The cats! Are they alright? I—"

"They're fine," he said with a soft chuckle, coming around the side of the bed just like the nurse had. "Mom's got them in a box, and I'm sure is doting on them. She's always had a thing for animals, although usually it's towards her chickens." Elizabeth opened her mouth to say something, but he cut her off. "And yes, she treats her chickens better than the pigs. They're her babies, and she takes care of them herself. They're not for profit or anything; I have the feeling the only reason Dad let her pour so much money into them was to get her a hobby that didn't include horses or any sort of gambling."

"Is, uh, is that a problem for your mother?"

"No, but it's not uncommon for housewives with too much money to develop bad habits." He frowned. "Now that I think about it, that sure does sound condescending when said out loud."

"Let me guess, something your father told you all?"

"Often and emphatically."

She chuckled lightly before taking a sip of her water. It helped wash down some of the filth in her mouth, which was nice, but she still grimaced at the taste.

"Are you alright? Can I get you anything? Are they letting you eat or drink?"

Another chuckle. "I'm fine. Just kinda piecing my world back together. Have a seat, please. Your standing is making me feel nervous."

"Alright then, if the lady insists."

She didn't take into account just how close that would bring him, and her heart skittered in her chest. That was about the last thing she needed at the moment, but she pushed through it.

"So," she started, after swallowing more water. "How did you find me?"

"Honestly, it was mostly luck. I nearly ran into your car and then when I got out, I heard the cat's yowling."

"She was pretty loud, wasn't she?"

"Well it worked. She got someone to come save her kitties."

Oh yeah, that was right. Elizabeth *had* managed to save them. Somehow, that made everything seem much less awful. Like all of it was worth it. ...even if she wasn't exactly clear on what all of "it" was at the moment.

"You sure your mom will be alright with them? Kittens that young are a lot."

"Hey, how about we worry about you right now, the human?"

Her eyes flashed. That was something someone said when a horrible thing happened. "They're *kittens*. I'm less fragile then they are."

He let out a sigh, reaching out to take her hand. She almost didn't notice the motion at first, but then his fingers were winding around hers, warm and calloused.

He didn't ask to touch her hand, and yet she didn't mind. There wasn't a threat to it or a declaration of ownership. It was just... a touch. A confirmation that she was real. And when she looked over at his face, she saw nothing but deep concern etched into his handsome features.

And... had he been *crying*?

She didn't think she had ever seen him look scared or even that uncertain. Sure, she'd managed to confuse him a few times, surprise him even, but he'd never looked so rattled to his core since the moment she'd met him almost two months ago.

And she realized, with a strange sort of uncurling warmth, that he felt that way because he thought *she* was hurt.

Oh.

Oh *wow.*

It was certainly a thought, and a heady one at that. It made her toes want to curl and her skin kind of itch. She instantly dismissed it, of course. He was just concerned about the liability of his family's insurance. He just cared about the fallout if his family found out that he not only hired a vet but then let her die on their grounds.

But as "realistic" as those thoughts might be, they just didn't match up with the expression on his face. An earnestness that she wasn't used to seeing. It seemed like he cared, really and truly cared that she was safe.

"They're safe with Mom. She's probably spoiling them rotten, in fact. She was training to be a nurse for a while, you know."

Elizabeth nodded, feeling embarrassed for having almost snapped at him. He was the man that had saved her life. Dragged her up from the ground and—oh goodness, had he *carried* her in the storm? She wasn't exactly a lightweight, and she'd had the cats with her too.

"Are..." She paused, licking her lips. Even with the water her mouth was so unbelievably dry. "Did you get hurt?"

He shook his head. "Just some windburn and a bruise on my shin. I'm fine. The nurse told me that you took a really hard blow to the back of your head. That's what they're running the tests on. Luckily the slice on your leg cleaned up really well."

"My leg?"

She turned her head enough to look down, lifting her leg at the same time, and sure enough there was a line of sutures there. "Oh. Right. A piece of metal sheeting slammed into me."

Sterling whistled quietly. "Metal sheeting? You're lucky you still have a leg."

She settled, laughing dryly. "You know, there isn't a lot about this situation that really feels lucky."

"Fair enough. Considering I didn't so much as get a rock in my face, I suppose we could question your fortune."

Another laugh, but smaller, and she paused to drink again. Her brain still felt fuzzy, but whenever she looked at Sterling, she felt her world shifting slightly. Like her perception of him was rebuilding, bit by bit, to have an entirely different picture of him.

"You're not so bad, you know that?" she said.

He sat up at that, looking back and forth as if he wasn't sure she was talking to him. But who else would she be talking to?

When she let out the slightest of chuckles, his cheeks colored, and he relaxed.

"I know a lot of people who would disagree with you," he said finally, something odd in his tone.

"Yeah, but those people weren't saved from bleeding out in a puddle in the middle of a storm."

"You wouldn't have—"

"Ah-ah," she held up a finger. "I'm being gracious and complimentary. This doesn't happen often, so just enjoy the moment."

His lips curled into a smile and wow, if that wasn't just a thing and a half to behold. God really wasn't pulling any punches when he made that Miller bone structure, was he?

"Alright, whatever you say, ma'am."

"Now you're talking," she said, letting herself relax further. Already she was exhausted, and her head was getting swimmy again. She wondered if she could take a nap before they came back for more tests...

14

Elizabeth

*E*lizabeth looked at the clock, her phone long dead. Actually, she wasn't sure if it was just a lack of charge or if all the water damage from it being in her pocket had caused it to die permanently. She supposed she would find out when she got home and plugged it into her charger.

Wait... was she supposed to put it in rice first just to be cautious? She couldn't quite remember. Although she had mostly come back to herself in the hours since she had arrived at the hospital, there was still a gentle sort of brain fog in her head, making it hard to think about things that weren't everyday issues.

But they had run all of their tests and seemed satisfied that she was safe to be released, so at least that was good. Unfortunately, it was two in the morning, too late to call any of her friends to ask for a ride, and she didn't really have the energy to drive back home if she made it to her car.

Oh, her *car!* She had forgotten that she'd left it basically in the middle of the work road, door open and still running. There was no way that it wasn't soaked and completely out of gas. Poor thing. As if her poor little junker needed anything else stacked up against it.

Granted, all the money she was getting on a biweekly basis had certainly helped her and her father a lot already. She was finally caught up with her bills, and they both had full fridges for once. Her tank had been consistently full for the first time in... well, since she had bought the old junker, and it was a nice feeling.

Maybe she could call some sort of rideshare thing? Wait, no, her phone was dead. Right. She had forgotten.

The nurse finished trundling her out to the waiting room, having insisted that she sit in a wheelchair while she was discharged, and she was surprised to see Sterling waiting right there. He had disappeared sometime while Elizabeth was sleeping, and she was sure that he'd gone home.

"You're still here?" she asked cautiously.

"Of course," he said, looking at her like it was strange to think that he would be anywhere else. "I had to use the restroom and then you were passed out, so I decided to take a walk rather than wake you. Parked my car in the garage too. By the time I came back, they told me you were being woken up and discharged, so I went back to the garage and got my car. Figured I'd just wait out here for you since they said you'd only be a couple of minutes."

He'd done all that for her while she was out? Maybe it wasn't *really* that much, but after years of taking care of herself, it boggled her mind that someone would jump through so many inconveniences just to make sure she had a ride.

Swallowing the strange rush of feelings that forced its way up her chest, she realized she could ask him for his phone so that she might at least call a taxi and not bother him anymore. But before she could vocalize even a single word, he was speaking again.

"*Oh man*, I just realized I should have asked one of my brothers to drive your car down once the storm cleared. I didn't even think of it."

"The storm cleared?" she asked, looking out the windows. But all she saw beyond the front lights of the hospital was darkness. Right, the emergency room faced two large industrial buildings that had been abandoned, cutting off almost all streetlights or other illumination. Not very cheery. Hopefully, those who had to stay overnight in the hospital had better views.

"Yeah, about a couple of hours ago. A lot of accidents, though. I'm not surprised the ER's been swamped the entire time we were here."

She looked around at the waiting room, where there were only about ten people or so. "It was?"

His responding chuckle was gentle, without a hint of teasing to it. "It's alright, you were preoccupied with other things. Now, where am I taking you?"

"Oh, my house isn't in this city. I live in a small town about thirty, forty minutes on the opposite side of your family's estate. Just take me to a hotel where I can power nap then take a taxi back to my car."

Sure, she would be without her phone for a while, but she would survive. She'd been in tougher scrapes. And she was relatively fine thanks to Sterling. She had been so sure that he was a selfish, self-involved rich boy, but he really had risked his life to go out there into a wild storm to save her. That was just about the exact *opposite* thing that he was supposed to do.

"A hotel?" He made a face, and she wasn't sure if she should be flattered or insulted. "I don't—I just—Uh, why don't you stay in one of our guest rooms? We have plenty, and Simon's wing is practically empty if you *really* want space. The only people you'd even run into would be our cleaning staff."

Elizabeth didn't answer right away, licking her lips nervously. It seemed like it was crossing another boundary, one that was very, *very* stark. And the last time she had even come close to the line, it had ended disastrously.

And even though she knew Sterling wouldn't hurt her, that he and his brother Silas had never once done anything untoward with her, she still couldn't shut off the worry that pretty much every woman had when staying somewhere strange.

"Or even my parent's wing, if you want," Sterling continued, his cheeks coloring in that way that was far more adorable than it had any right to be.

She thought about it, her weary mind trying to slug through the risks of it, but eventually she decided to risk it. After all, Sterling had gone out into a storm where he could have had a limb chopped off by a piece of metal. He'd then driven through that same storm to get her to help. It was pretty unlikely that he would do all of those things just to molest her in some grand and elaborate scheme.

...or, at least she hoped so? Why was it so hard for her to trust people?

"Alright, that sounds like it might be the best plan. I can rest up as much as I need then head out when I'm collected."

The smile on his face looked like it could have illuminated the whole hospital for a few hours. "Really? Great. It makes me feel better knowing you'll be one hundred percent yourself. You're far too agreeable when you're not yourself, you know that?"

She scoffed. "I'm pretty sure that was just an insult."

"But I meant it in the most complimentary way." He offered her his arm and she took it, feeling steadied by his strength. His warmth.

They headed outside, his steps slow and measured for her. It wasn't something that she normally needed, but she was grateful for it, considering that she felt like a fawn taking its first few steps.

If he noticed her shakiness, he had the decency to not say so and was soon helping her get situated in his truck. While she allowed him to give her a hand up and make sure she didn't hit her head, she drew the line at him buckling the seat belt for her.

"I'm not a complete invalid."

"Sorry," he said with a rueful grin, which was just about as unfair as his other grins. "Didn't mean to mother hen you." He closed the door for her and then walked around the front. As he popped into his side, he looked over. "Sorry if the seat is a bit damp. I cleaned it best I could while you were out, but I really thought they were gonna keep you here until sunrise."

"You cleaned it?" she asked before she looked down at her recently cleaned clothes. Someone had taken them and washed them for her while she was in her hospital gown. She could have been wrong, but she was pretty sure that was a service that wasn't normally provided for patients. Especially not patients who were never admitted.

Strange.

She side-eyed Sterling as he pulled backward then towards the road. Had he asked them for her clothes and then taken them to a laundromat? She didn't think she was out *that* long. But then again, the nurse had told her they'd made him wait out in the general area for the first couple hours she was there. That was the procedure because Elizabeth had to give her consent before he could be in the room.

She could just ask him, but for some reason she didn't want to. Maybe it was because she didn't know how to say the words without sounding accusatory. Maybe it was because she wouldn't know what to do if he said no. It'd be weird... right? So instead she just said nothing.

But that seemed to be just fine because Sterling was talking pretty much as soon as they got on the wide, four-lane road that would lead them to the highway.

"How are you feeling, by the way?"

"Fine," Elizabeth answered out of habit before realizing she owed him a more complete answer. He had risked his life for her, after all. "Tired, that's for sure. And my head is a little achy, and I'm feeling a little bit out there from whatever medicine they gave me. Kind of like a storm in the distance."

He wrinkled his nose at that. "How about no more storms for a while? I think I've had my fill."

"Hah, you better find somewhere else to live then."

He cracked a grin. "You may have a point."

"I've been known to have those once in a while."

"What a humble way to say that you're always right."

Her laugh surprised her, tumbling out of her mouth so easily. "I really am, aren't I?"

"Well," he said with a mock-serious tone. "I suppose that depends on who you ask."

"Nah, they'll say I was always right too, they just didn't like that I was."

"You sound like you're talking from experience."

She leveled him with a look. "Oh, you don't even know."

"I suppose I don't, really."

His words took on a thoughtful sort of tone that Elizabeth didn't have it into her to sort. It didn't help that she was feeling a bit nauseous from the city lights flashing by. Closing her eyes, she let her head loll back against the seat. Although it was clean and not damp at all, she was pretty sure that she smelled the tiniest scent of earth and rain.

Huh, not only had she ruined his clothes—he still had mud caked into his shirt and some of his pants—she also had messed up his truck. She knew that for some men their rides were practically their children, but he didn't even seem to care.

Curiouser and curiouser.

"You okay over there?"

"Yeah, just a little dizzy from things whipping by. I think I'll leave my eyes closed."

"Do you need me to lower a window? Turn on some music? Or would that hurt?"

He was being so thoughtful, so careful. It was strange, and she couldn't tell if it seemed so significant because she was still messed up from her injury or if it was as meaningful as it felt in the moment. Could a head injury make her sappy? Was sappiness a legitimate medical symptom?

Who knew? Maybe she'd ask a doctor the next day.

"Music would be nice, I think," she answered instead, realizing that she had been quiet for longer than what was usual. "As long as it's low."

"Sure. Let me see, I think I got something that would work. Can you plug my phone in? Code is 1920."

"1920?" she asked, skipping over her incredulousness that he was not only trusting her with his personal device but that he also gave her the password to it. "That mean something?"

"You'll laugh."

"Considering the day that I've had, would that be such a bad thing?"

He glanced over to her as much as he could, considering that he was driving, but she just blinked blankly at him. If he thought that he could outlast her deadpan, he had another thing coming. She'd learned it from her mother, and she'd brought a whole room in a fraternity party to a standstill with a five-minute glare.

Sterling didn't last five minutes, however, and after maybe one and a half, he huffed. "Fine. If you're so curious, it's based off the first Bible verses I memorized."

"Really?" she asked, her eyebrows going up. She didn't know why she was surprised to hear the boy was, at one point, a Christian. Maybe it was because she was so used to rich people worshiping at the altar of money, gain and power, which was pretty much the opposite of what Jesus was all about. "You were a Christian?"

"*Am* a Christian," he corrected, sounding somewhere between mildly offended and surprised. "Did you not know?"

"Nope. I'm not super familiar with your family, but none of you really come off that way." She could feel him staring at her with all of his non-driving attention, but she just closed her eyes and re-assumed her resting position.

"We don't?" he said finally.

"It was stupid. Never mind. I took a blow to the head, you know."

But it was clear he wasn't ready to drop it. "Out of the mouths of babes and those with concussions come the truth."

"That is *not* how that phrase goes."

"*Elizabeth.*"

Ugh, why did he have to say her name like that? It was firm, but there was a sort of pleading to it that made her heart thump in her chest. Made it thump *hard*. Quickly she noted to herself to ask the doctor about heart thumpiness along with sappiness.

"I dunno, it's just your massive castle-mansion is kinda not what Jesus was into, you know? And the fact that you've got so much money into possessions instead of taking care of humans or your animals.

"And I'm not saying it's wrong to have nice things. I *like* nice things. I've just noticed that those who have *so* much money usually got there by stepping on other people's heads. I mean, how many times over could your family feed the poor of the city and still be fine? And yet... people are still going hungry, aren't they?"

Sterling didn't say anything for several long moments, and she inwardly berated herself. Why couldn't she keep her mouth shut?

"I never thought about it that way."

"Why would you? I assume you were born with wealth. When it's there all your life, how do you know that it's not what's normal?"

She opened her eyes just enough to peek at him, and she saw a wan smile cross his features.

"Is this why you haven't been talking to me for the past month and a half?" he asked.

That startled her enough into opening both of her eyes. "What?"

"You've been avoiding me. Ever since that lunch we were supposed to enjoy together in the city."

"You mean the one where you rubbed in my face the fact that you could solve my problems instantly while I was drowning in them?" Oh no, she shouldn't have said that that way either. She needed to never get hit in the head again because it was clearly getting her into trouble.

"I..." He paused for several beats.

She watched as his tongue flicked out to wet his lips. He had... *really* nice lips and for a moment, she wondered if he understood just how pretty he was. He had to, right?

"I didn't remember it that way," he said.

"Of course, you didn't. To you, it was insane to have such a tiny little blip cause so much trouble. To you, it was an easy fix. I maybe didn't react the best. I just... My dad always said I was far too independent for my own good, so when you just flippantly said you'd pay it like it was no big deal, I couldn't help but feel like you were, I dunno, condescending. Saying you were better than me.

"And it kinda confirmed to me that there needed to be a distance between us. After all, you're my boss and I'm your employee. You're rich and I'm poor. You're wh—" She cut herself off, not sure she could go that far.

"I'm a white guy born to a legacy, and you're an African American woman," he finished for her, surprising her that he knew where her mind had been heading. "I know I may not come across as the most cultured guy, but I know that contains some hurdles I'll never have to go through."

"I want to say that I'm not surprised to hear you say that, but wow, I really am."

She hadn't been prepared to have such a deep, meaningful conversation while she was concussed, but she couldn't find the self-restraint to tie her tongue anyway.

"Yeah, I'm beginning to wonder exactly the sort of impression I give of myself," Sterling said, his words clearly only half a joke.

"I'm sorry."

"What do you have to be sorry for? You're just being truthful."

"I dunno. You saved my life. You've given me a job. I don't want to sound ungrateful. I just—" She breathed in and out, gathering her words. They were so slippery around her thoughts, flitting this way and that, hard to collect in the order that she wanted. "I guess I've never been too good at sugarcoating my words, and I'm even less good about it right now."

He shook his head. "You don't need to sugarcoat anything for me. If anything, I think maybe people have been doing that around my family too much." He frowned, his free hand that wasn't on the steering wheel stroking his chin thoughtfully. "Huh."

"That was a thoughtful *huh*. What'cha thinking?"

"Just about conversations I've been having with my brothers over the past few months."

"Like what?"

But he just shook his head again. "Another time maybe. It's not important. Let's listen to that music. Why don't you search for an album called *Night Bliss*?"

Night Bliss? That sounded risky. But she searched for it anyway and clicked on it once it popped up. A moment later the aux cord did its work, and she was surprised when beautiful, borderline haunting violins began to gently play.

Oh.

The melody drifted in gentle waves, other stringed instruments joining one by one. It reminded her of the ocean, building and receding, growing and shrinking, laying one on top of each other in ways that were both relaxing and inspiring.

"What is this?"

"Some newer age orchestral music. I was introduced to it in college. This particular band is comprised only of the blind."

"It's *beautiful*," she whispered. When he didn't respond for several long moments, she looked over at him again to see that he was staring at her.

"Yeah. It is."

Hmm… if she didn't know better, she'd think with the way he was looking at her that he maybe thought it was more than just the music that was beautiful.

THEY GOT through about half of the album before they arrived, and Elizabeth was almost tempted to just sit there and keep listening. But she was also so exhausted that it was hard to keep her eyes open.

"I texted my mom during one of the times you nodded off on the ride," Sterling said as he helped her out of his truck. When she gave him a dirty look for that, he chuckled lightly. "Don't worry, I used all voice commands to send it. Didn't even take my hands off the wheel."

Huh. Rich-people technology was wild.

"Anyway, she's left some stuff out for you so you can sleep more comfortably and have a change of clothes."

"Oh, that was nice of her."

He gave an absent sort of nod, but right as he helped her to the ground, his stomach let out a truly egregious growl.

"Whoa, is there a dog growling around here or are you just *that* hungry?"

Even in the dark she could see the top of those chiseled cheekbones flushing slightly. "I guess that I was so worried before that I didn't really take the time to eat. I'll be fine."

She nodded, but then she realized that the last time she ate was just a cold cut sandwich at noon the previous day, and now she was absolutely *starving*.

"You know what, I wouldn't mind a midnight snack."

"You mean a four in the morning snack?"

"I'm too hungry to care what the correct time is. Feed me, please, and thanks."

He laughed outright at that, and she found that she liked the sound more and more. "Look at you, being right again. Alright, think you can make it to the kitchen?"

She sent him another glare, and there was that laugh again. Of course, her heart felt that need to do that *thing* again and she felt her cheeks color. Goodness. She hoped that whatever was going on with her brain calmed down by the next day or work was going to be *real* awkward.

"Right, right, sorry. No mother-henning. This way."

Although he did lead her, he didn't remove his arm from her hold, which she appreciated. She probably could have gotten along fine without it, but it made her feel secured. Less likely to stumble. She wasn't used to having to worry about such things, her strides always sure and precise. Her friend had once said she walked like someone people didn't want to get in the way of, cruising down the college halls, anxious to get to her next class so she could squeeze in more time reading. There was certainly nothing intense about her slightly stilted gait now.

They made it to the kitchen without any mishaps or sudden trip-ups, however, and Elizabeth found herself being helped up onto one of the very comfortable looking stools at the kitchen island.

Except it was so much more than an island, it was practically big enough to serve as a raft if there was a flood. And everything about the kitchen was new and shiny. Chrome,

chrome, chrome everywhere for the appliances with a beautiful and fancy sort of rack above the ovens—yeah, oven*s*, as in *plural*—with all sorts of expensive-looking pans hanging from it.

Yet, despite the evident newness of it, the state of the art of it all, there was still a very homey feel to it. The walls were a light white, the countertops were marble but had wooden accents that were polished to a high shine. There was a huge window with translucent white, luxurious curtains, and she could just imagine the sunlight pouring in during the day.

And so many *plants*.

Hanging from those were cute little woven baskets, on shelves, basically anywhere there was space and it wouldn't crowd. She saw aloes, two bonsai trees that she knew had to cost a pretty penny. There were hanging vine plants. Spider plants. Christmas cactuses. Fancy looking ferns, peace lilies and others that she didn't even know the names of. All of it put together was so welcoming that she could almost forget that she was in the kitchen of her mega-rich employer and the room alone was probably worth more than her entire apartment building combined.

"I don't think I have it in me to cook something. How about some sandwiches?"

Even though she'd had the exact same thing at lunch, she was willing to bet that Sterling's supplies were a lot different from cheap bologna on basic sliced cheese that came individually wrapped in little plastic sheets. "Yeah, sandwiches sound good."

"You got a preference? I have roast beef, corned beef, some grilled chicken, chorizo and *soppressata*."

"Soap and what now?" she asked, catching herself on that last word.

"I'm feeling roast beef. Roast beef and maybe some Havarti? Or pepperjack."

"Pepperjack," Elizabeth said like she had any authority on the matter. And yet Sterling seemed pleased as punch at her suggestion.

"Pepperjack it is then."

He went about making the sandwiches and she watched him load *way* more meat than she would ever allow herself. Although her financial situation was quickly changing due to being paid well for the first time since ever, she still had a lifetime of being frugal and pinching pennies to make ends meet. She didn't know how long it would take her to be able to pile on cold cut after cold cut like Sterling was doing, but she had a feeling she might never get there.

"You got any food allergies I should worry about while I'm over here handling things?" he asked over his shoulder, a look of concentration on his face that should not have been as endearing as it was.

"Nope. Just allergic to bee stings and a couple of detergents."

"Detergents, really?"

She nodded. "Found out once on a school trip to NYC. Had an awful case of hives from the sheets."

"Well, I promise, no detergent in this sandwich."

"That's a relief," she said with a smirk.

He crossed to her, placing a truly thick sandwich down in front of her. She was used to Texas toast, naturally, but whatever bread he had used was even thicker and fluffier looking. Probably some of that specialty stuff that she could never justify looking at, let alone buying.

Or maybe Mrs. Miller made it? Elizabeth was pretty sure she recognized what was maybe the fanciest mixer she'd ever seen in the corner of the kitchen. And Sterling himself had said that she didn't work.

Oh man, Elizabeth couldn't remember the last time she'd had homemade bread, so she hastily picked it up and took her first bite. And it only took that single bite for her eyes to practically roll up into the back of her head and an embarrassing groan to force its way past her very full mouth.

"That good?" Sterling asked.

He was trying to play it off, but she could practically see his pride was perking up at her obvious appreciation. But as she thought about it, she wondered how much the middle son of an empire, who messed up a big engagement thing on top of everything else, actually felt appreciated.

"You know it," she said, words still muffled around her food. Normally she would never talk with her mouth full, but the levity seemed right in the moment. She liked seeing Sterling smile. A real smile. Not any of his manufactured—but still devastatingly effective—smiles that he was used to whipping out to charm people.

"Careful, you might make a gentleman blush."

"Oh yeah? Well I'll be real careful if I see a gentleman around."

He pressed his hand to his chest, giving her an affronted look. "You wound me, madam!"

"Mademoiselle, technically. And if you want to go to the hospital for that, then you're just going to have to call an ambulance. I'm tapped out, I'm afraid."

"The cheek," he huffed, although she could see his grin trying to peek out of his act.

He took a giant bite of his sandwich, and the two of them happily sat in the quiet while they chewed. Elizabeth couldn't remember the last time that she'd had so much fun bantering with someone. She wasn't sure if it was the head injury or that she was just so exhausted that she couldn't hold her normal guard up, but either way it was nice. Really, really *nice*.

"This day turned out different than I expected," she said. "I thought you were going to fire me."

Sterling swallowed. "What's this about firing you?"

"I've been expecting you to fire me any day now," she said, pointing what was left of her sandwich at him.

"Why would I do that? Don't you know this is all a plot to emotionally indebt you to me so that you never leave, and you just stick around here forever, improving all of our animals' lives until they have perfect existences?"

She snorted at that. "Like that is even believable."

A strange sort of look crossed over his handsome features, but then he was gently chuckling too. "I guess maybe it's not so believable with the way it seems like you view me."

Oh, she didn't like that look. She didn't like that look at *all*.

Reaching out, she gently laid her hand over his. They had never touched so much in such a small amount of time, never even *talked* so much, but she wanted to comfort him. Despite their differences, she didn't like seeing him in pain.

"I really appreciate everything you've done for me, and everything you're doing for your animals. You could have just turned me away. You didn't have to do any of that."

Despite her hope that her words would make him feel better, he seemed to grow more uncomfortable. "You shouldn't have had to correct so much stuff in the first place."

"Maybe not. But I've found that it's not so much the mistakes we make that define us, but how we choose to correct them. If we choose to correct them at all."

There it was, the slightest of smiles sliding in to replace his dubious expression. "That's a pretty thing to say."

"It's a true thing to say."

He nodded, and they finished the last of their sandwiches. She was surprised when he placed their dirty plates on the counter, but at her concerned look, he shrugged and said something about their cleaning staff.

Right, the Millers were so rich that they hired people to do their basic housekeeping for them. How did they not run around bored all of the time? If she didn't have to work to survive, didn't have to tidy her place and run errands, she would have far too much free time on her hands.

But of course, she didn't say any of that as he led her up a flight of stairs and then down a long hall and around another corner. It almost reminded her of being in some sort of very strangely arranged hotel. Although the place was clearly carefully and meticulously decorated with many expensive things, there wasn't any *soul* to it. No life. It was a manicured landscape of wealth, but she knew nothing else about the family it was supposed to contain. Certainly, their whole personalities couldn't just be that they had money. Sterling was a character for sure.

"So which of your brother's space am I crashing?"

"Simon. He's finishing up his last year of college right now. You'll definitely get a chance to meet him before we finish everything you want to do with the pigs."

"And maybe your other animals," she added hopefully.

"We'll see."

Not the answer she had been hoping for, but certainly one that she had been expecting. Oh well. She didn't have much time to pout about that, however, as she heard the gentle mewling of kittens.

"Is this me?" she asked, pointing to the cracked door the noise was coming from.

"Yup. One of his guest bedrooms. It's a little spartan, but it's quiet, and he always insisted on an obscene number of pillows so you should be comfy. Say hi to the cats for me. I'm pretty sure Mom's already in love with all of them."

It was all just so *much*. She felt like she was nearly overwhelmed with all of it. From their house to him saving her, to the way his eyes flashed when he was joking with her and how easily he kept up with her banter. He was so much *more* than she'd allowed herself to believe, and she was beginning to wonder why she had judged him so harshly.

She didn't know what came over her, but before she knew it, she was standing on her tiptoes and pressing a soft kiss to the man's cheek. It was nothing, a chaste little peck, and yet her senses felt even more overloaded than they were before. His masculine scent filled her nose and the rough stubble of his face scratched at her sensitive skin, but somehow not in a bad way. She lingered perhaps a beat longer than she should have before stepping back.

"Thank you for being there for me," she murmured sheepishly before retreating into the room. But as she closed the door, she couldn't bring herself to regret her rash action. She just wanted him to know that, despite her prickliness, he had a friend in her.

It was the least she could do for someone who had saved her life.

15

Sterling

*S*terling was floating.

Or at least it felt like he was floating.

For perhaps the hundredth time, his hand went to his cheek right where Elizabeth's soft and full lips had pressed themselves two nights earlier. Of course, he couldn't feel anything different there, that wasn't possible, and yet he still felt like he could feel the burning outline of her mouth.

Which, naturally, was absolutely absurd. It was just a kiss on the cheek. Chaste. Innocent. More salacious things happened in the Sunday comics. And yet he was floating, nonetheless.

It had been three days since he'd seen her last, and as he readied in the morning, he found he was itching to talk to her again. He'd been in such a panic driving her to the hospital that he'd been practically outside of himself, not thinking about anything but getting her to safety. But once the doctors told her that she would be fine, that she just needed a few days rest and general monitoring—as well as another check up on that leg in a week or two—he finally found himself able to think. To *breathe.* To answer the question of why seeing the woman laid out on the ground had scared him down to his core.

But what he hadn't expected was for her to be so *fun,* so witty afterward. He expected her to revert to her somewhat callous, coldly professional treatment of him. But instead she was warm, and snarky, and he suddenly felt much more engaged than he had in a long time.

And then she'd *kissed* him... and even thought it was just an innocent kiss on the cheek, it was like his world turned upside down.

He shook his head, trying to make himself focus as he washed his face in the mirror. But his thoughts went to how he'd told her to go home for the weekend and take Monday off. He'd wanted to spend more time with her, to bind her up in blankets and make sure that nothing hurt her ever again, but he knew that wasn't his place. Sure, she had kissed him on the cheek, but she'd done that out of gratitude, a kind gesture from someone who had been through a lot. It didn't mean that he had any sort of right to her.

But he *had* paid for her car to be cleaned out starting in the early morning, and she only had to wait around about an hour after she had woken up, claiming she never usually slept in so late. But then she was driving home, and he was left to soak in all of his racing thoughts.

He was glad that she had refused to accept his offer to give her the whole week off—paid, of course. She said that she would go crazy from the boredom, but secretly he couldn't help but be a bit selfishly pleased.

His phone beeped at him, reminding him that he'd been in the bathroom for more than ten minutes and was about to run late if he wanted to catch Elizabeth before she plunged into her work. He knew that he was spending a lot of extra time getting ready, but... well... he wanted to make a good impression.

Which, again, was not like him.

Nevertheless, he finished getting ready and headed out, checking his reflection in his rearview mirror about twice on the drive over to the pens. When he got there, he was surprised to see no Elizabeth, but his twin was there instead. When he slid out of his truck, Silas gave him a knowing look.

Which, naturally, Sterling chose to ignore. Whatever his twin was thinking was wrong. Even if their twin thing made it so neither of them were ever usually wrong at all when it came to what the other was thinking.

He made the conscious choice to walk past his older twin, but when he went inside, he was surprised to see his mother was standing there right next to Elizabeth, both of them talking and laughing, looking like they were having a great conversation.

...what?

Sterling looked at his phone, making sure he hadn't accidentally set his alarms for much later than he thought, but nope, it was about fifteen minutes before she was supposed to start working. Why was everyone around? Obviously, Silas had driven Mom to see the pens, but the question was *why*?

Wondering if he was in some sort of strange dream, he approached the two women cautiously. But Mom just put her hand on Elizabeth's shoulder, squeezing in that comforting way that only a mom could do.

"I don't know what's suddenly happened to have so many

lovely young women in my life at once, but I love it! You are a gem, aren't you?"

Elizabeth's dark cheeks colored slightly with her blush, and if that wasn't just a right pretty sight. "I don't know about that, ma'am, but thank you."

"Don't try to play it off, I'm an excellent judge of character. You should come see my garden at the manor! I bet you would love it." Of course, his Mom would jump at the chance to show someone else her pride and joy—besides her chickens. She'd even roped Teddy into helping her more often than not with the planting, upkeep and everything else that went into growing prize-winning vegetables.

"I bet I would. How about I swing by at my afternoon break?"

"Of course! Now, I suppose I should get started on my day. I have quite the to-do list. I'll see you later, Miss Brown."

"That sounds great, Mrs. Miller."

His mom nodded then practically skipped to Sterling. Granted it wasn't an *actual* skip, but there was certainly plenty of bounce to her step as she crossed the barn floor. She stood on tiptoe, kissing Sterling's other cheek. Goodness, was there something in the air?

"Hello, son. Good to see you up and at 'em. You've been so busy lately!"

"You know me," he said weakly. "Trying to stay occupied."

"Right, right. Maybe you could swing by with Miss Brown during the afternoon. Wouldn't hurt you to spend more time with your poor old mother, right?"

Where was that coming from? "Of course, Mom. Whatever you say."

She nodded then trundled out, no doubt to race off in her pink go-kart that Teddy had decorated even more. Sterling was pretty sure that his Mom took pleasure in making each of her sons drive her around in her pastel Barbie dream-kart.

Sterling waited until she was gone before he turned to Elizabeth. "Whatever she told you, I assure you that it was an absolute lie."

"Oh, so you're telling me that you didn't have night terrors as a child if you didn't sleep with your favorite stuffed cowboy doll?"

"Lies. Lies and slander."

"Uh-huh, I'm sure." Elizabeth's smile was saccharinely sweet and dripping with sarcasm, but he loved it. It made her features light up and his heart thunder in his chest. "And I'm sure you didn't also cry when you found out Santa, the Tooth Fairy and the Easter Bunny were all fake on the same day."

"You know what, that was a very traumatic time of my life."

She laughed, her full lips pulling away from her teeth as she laughed. It was such a difference from the gated-off, composed woman he was used to. The one that only spoke to him when necessary and never anything more than a few words at a time. It made her dark, almond eyes light up and her face open like the sun parting through dark clouds. He liked it. He liked it a *lot*. He didn't know what he would give to make sure that she always wore such a happy expression, but it was a lot.

Or maybe everything?

No, it wouldn't do any good to go overboard.

"I'm sure. It's a testament that you're a functional adult, really."

"You know... I'm thinking we should try that whole after-negotiation meal thing over again," he blurted without thinking, the words issuing faster than his brain could keep up.

But she didn't even blink. "You think so? I thought you said that we should wait a bit further into the pigpen development before we moved on to other animals."

That... that wasn't what Sterling meant at all.

He realized quickly that she thought he was just being friendly, just extending the banter between the two of him, but that suddenly wasn't enough. Sterling had been lost for a long time. Listless with no real direction. But he was absolutely certain now that he wanted Elizabeth more than he had ever wanted anything else in his life.

"No, I didn't mean like—I'm not—" He took a breath, centering himself. "I meant as a date. A dinner, between you and me."

"A *date?*"

Although she parroted his words, she didn't say anything else, just stared at him with huge eyes. He found very quickly that he didn't like that at all, and he felt panic start to rise in him. "Of course, you don't—"

"Is that appropriate considering that you're my employer?"

His stomach dropped at that, and he found himself quickly searching for an answer. "Well, technically it's McLintoc Ranch, LLC, that's your employer. I just happen to be related to the guy that owns the place."

"And the guy whose expense account my paycheck is coming from."

She... had a point there. He didn't like it, but she had a point.

"If that bothers you, I understand. I just thought—"

"A dinner together would be nice."

What—did she...

"As long as it's not at that one place, and I'll drive myself," she added.

He knew he was smiling *way* too broadly, but he couldn't help it. "Sounds like a deal."

16

Elizabeth

*E*lizabeth pulled up to the nice restaurant that Sterling had given her the name of, and she couldn't help but feel intimidated.

Which, of course, was absolutely not like her at all. Nothing intimidated Elizabeth. She was determined, headstrong, and driven, or at least that was what she had been told by people who *liked* her. But even those that didn't like her called her cocky or stubborn as some expletive or another. Point being, none of those words lent themselves to *intimidated* and yet that was exactly what she was.

The restaurant was some sort of fancy Italian place that she couldn't pronounce the name of. Apparently, she always pronounced everything with a Spanish accent, but it wasn't her fault that she'd started those second language classes when she was in fourth grade and continued them until she graduated college.

Okay... maybe it was a little her fault for taking Spanish as an elective four years straight, but whatever, at least she was fluent. It certainly helped her more than being able to pronounce fettucine or ricotta without an accent from below the border.

Whatever, she was just grateful it wasn't one of the few *really* high-end places from the rich side of the city, ones that needed a reservation and knowing someone on the inside to get in. If Sterling had suggested that, she might have just refused entirely.

But apparently, he'd thought about it a little, and so she'd agreed.

Sliding out of her car, she spotted Sterling already standing towards the front, the cut of his shoulders standing in sharp relief against the setting sun.

It was like something out of a movie poster, illuminating him in a soft light that made him look even more attractive than he or anyone else had any right to. He was wearing a light blue button-up and dark slacks, his hair brushed back into gentle waves atop his head. He wasn't quite wearing cowboy boots, but the cut of his shoes hinted at the same sort of feel.

He really did look like a cowboy. She wondered what he looked like atop a horse; face flushed as he raced across the fields of his estate. Maybe she'd find a way to wander over to the stables and see exactly how he handled his mount.

... or maybe she should try to get through the date first.

"Hey there," she said, approaching him with what she hoped was her usual, confident strut.

"Hey there," he said, looking at her almost *too* intensely.

"You look..." He hesitated as if he was cutting off whatever he was going to say and replaced it with something else. "...nice."

"What a coincidence, nice is what I was going for," she said with a chuckle, hoping that would ease him. He looked a bit nervous, for all his assured posture, and she understood how that felt.

Which was why she hadn't dressed to the nines. She was wearing a cute black pencil skirt her mother had picked out for her and a red, polka dot top with a ruffle. She'd taken the extra time to do her hair and makeup, which involved a long, seven-hour process that started the night previous. It was put together, it had a little flare, but it wasn't a five-star-dining-experience kind of outfit.

"Shall we go in?" he asked with that crooked smile of his.

"Let's," she said, taking his offered arm.

Together they walked in, and she tried not to ogle as they were greeted by the hostess and escorted to their table. It was definitely fancy inside, and she was beginning to wonder if her outfit was still far too underdressed for the situation.

If it was, Sterling didn't say, and soon they were sitting across from each other, a filigreed, pretty menu below her fingers.

"Do you have any recommendations?" she asked, almost licking her lips before she remembered that she was wearing a ruby-colored lipstick.

"What, you're telling me the professional Elizabeth Brown needs someone else's advice?"

"Hey," she said, grateful for him opening the floor with banter. She liked banter. Banter was comfortable. "I'll have you know, I'm happy to get advice from someone when they're more knowledgeable than me."

"Ah, but that must be a rare occurrence."

"You know, I'm very aware that you are teasing me, but I don't even care. Please, feed my ego."

He laughed again in that, not loud, but a low, rumbling sort of sound that flowed over the table like water. She liked it, but she wanted to make him tilt his head back like he had before and let out a real bellow. Maybe it was because he was always so composed, always so smooth, that she liked being able to take him apart like that. To make him show a true emotion, unfiltered and open.

"Bet you didn't know this was going to be a meal that fed you in more ways than one," he said.

"Ah yes, an inflated stomach and an inflated ego, the best of both worlds."

"I aim to please."

"I bet you do."

He opened his mouth, smirking at her as if he was going to say something especially saucy, but suddenly their server seemed to pop out of nowhere and greeted them.

Elizabeth tried not to lurch back, but her adrenaline spiked. She managed to recover before it was her time to order a drink, but once the server was gone, she couldn't help but blush a bit. Not for the first time, she was grateful that her darker skin stopped her complexion from ever going to bright pink.

"Maybe we should actually look at the menu this time," Sterling said, looking rueful as well.

"Goodness, and here I was just getting used to you buttering me up."

He laughed that quiet laugh once more, not enough for the feeling that was growing in her middle. "You know, you're a lot less scary when you're not saving an animal's life."

She cocked her eyebrow, leaning to post her chin in her hand. "So, I was scary, was I?"

"Terrifying," he confirmed. "I think some of our workers fled for the hills and never came back."

"Their bloodlines were weak," she said without missing a beat.

And there it was, that big, bellowing laugh. One of his hands went to his chest as he tilted his head back and let it out. He startled a few people, but neither of them cared. In fact, if someone asked her, she would say that the world didn't exist much beyond that sound.

"You're something else, you know that?" Sterling said.

"Always have been," she said before sobering slightly. "It's just that so many people aren't comfortable with what that *else* is."

She didn't know why she went there, but his face grew serious too. "What do you mean?"

"Ever feel like people expect certain things of you, and when you turn out to be different, you're disappointing them somehow?"

"...I can't remember the last time anyone expected anything from me. Maybe with Maddie and Val? And that was pretty mixed considering succeeding by them meant failing by my family."

Elizabeth let out a breath. "Strangely enough, I think I know what you mean."

"Do you?" he did look surprised at that, but she didn't let that put her off.

"Yeah. I just... growing up a black, poor kid in the south, I felt like I was always disappointing someone. I was a book nerd, and I applied myself to school more than anything else. It was really my whole world. Some of my peers got it, but a lot of them mocked me. Called me an 'Oreo.'"

"An Oreo?"

"You know, I may be black on the outside, but I'm really white on the inside."

She almost expected him to laugh it off, but instead those incredible lips of his pulled down into a frown. "That seems pretty cruel."

"It was. But I never really fit in with white folks either. I'm lucky that we live in the time we do, but there's still... you know, plenty of stuff. Being told that I spoke so well, that I was surprisingly articulate. That I was an *example* for others. And of course, I remember I was in a tight competition for valedictorian with this other girl. She was brilliant, really. But her family was loaded—not compared to y'all, of course—and she could afford all sorts of tutors that I couldn't. When I managed to beat her by a tenth of a percent, she said clearly I was an 'affirmative action pick.'" She huffed. "Like that existed."

"I'm sorry."

"You're alright. You weren't there. Kids are cruel. People are cruel. I'm glad we live in an age where more people are loving and accepting than people aren't, but man, the people who aren't sure do seem to have a lot of the power."

That frown deepened. "I guess I never thought about it."

She shrugged, looking down at the menu. "I don't know why I even brought it up. Not exactly dinner conversation."

But then his hand was cautiously sliding towards her, resting over hers. It was strange, his tanned but comparatively pale hand over hers. She'd never really thought about how their tones contrasted, complementing each other in their differences.

"I know it's weird, but I'm glad you did." When she looked up at him curiously, he swallowed then explained further. "I'm used to manicured conversations and plenty of posturing. I can feel people measuring their words when they talk to me. I like that you're not doing that anymore. It makes talking to you..."

"Yeah?"

Another pause before he answered. "It makes talking to you feel real."

There was a slight flutter in her chest, one that made her glow with pride. "I like to think that I'm real. Or at least I've always tried to be."

"I think you might be one of the most real people I know."

She didn't know what to say to that, which was also rare for her. Sterling seemed to be a series of new experiences for her, one right after the other, and she wasn't used to being so off-center.

But she also was quickly finding that she didn't hate it. It was new. It was exciting. She was so used to holding life with such a tightly dictated grip that it was almost a relief to relax her fingers and not know what was coming next.

"So, what do you recommend here?"

Sterling looked like he wanted to pursue it, push it further, but he must have changed his mind because he cleared his throat and answered her. "You know, you can't go wrong with the veal cannelloni."

"I'm not sure I'm really into sweets."

"Excuse me?"

His strange response had her blinking at him. "What you said, isn't that a dessert? With ricotta cheese or something? Fried?"

Sterling looked like he was trying very hard not to laugh. "Are you talking about a *cannoli*?"

She was still blinking at him. "Isn't that what you just said?"

"I'm sorry, I'm not making fun of you. That's just, just...

really more adorable than it should be. I was suggesting the veal *cannelloni*, not a dessert *cannoli*."

"Oh." She felt that same flush to her cheeks. "Well this is embarrassing."

"Don't worry about it. I guess now I can say that I'm the one that taught the great Elizabeth Brown something."

"I don't know about 'great.'"

"I do."

And she blushed harder. His fingers laced through hers and she relaxed her hand, allowing them to intertwine. There was a strange sort of sparking in her chest, a heat to her skin that she wasn't familiar with. She felt... she felt... *excited.*

But with the same unfortunate timing as before, the waiter returned with their drinks, a bottle of wine that Elizabeth hadn't even noticed that Sterling had ordered, and then asked if they were ready to order.

She haltingly got exactly what Sterling recommended, with him ordering something else that she couldn't really pronounce, and then it was just the two of them.

She understood that a moment had just happened, with their fingers intertwined. And Teddy's words played in her head.

Don't fall in love.

Was that what was happening? She'd always assumed that kind of thing wasn't for her, or if it was, it would be in her forties after some sort of meet-cute in a grocery store. She was dedicated to her degree, her father, getting financially stable, and of course to the animals.

But there was a strangeness in her that she couldn't name. It was fizzing and sparking and terrifying and wonderful. Small, of course, so small, but she kept feeling it grow. Part of her couldn't help but wonder if it was just because he saved her life. No one had done that for her, and she had sure seen plenty of movies dedicated to handsome heroes sweeping women off their feet. But it felt like more than that. Something deeper.

Something so very, *very* fragile.

But, as with all things that were delicate, it felt like whatever was growing within her could be crushed at any moment. In fact, if she wanted, she could probably crush it herself.

She didn't want to, though, or at least... she didn't think so.

Yet.

17

Sterling

*E*lizabeth was beautiful.

Like unearthly, unfairly, *impossibly* beautiful.

Of course, he'd always thought she was attractive, even covered in pig muck on the farm or with her face scrunched up in displeasure. But seeing her with her curls out all around her head, thick and shining, with ruby-red lips and darkly lined eyes... well, he had not been properly prepared.

And that wasn't even touching on her outfit. It was demure, some would even call it prudish, but it had his heart beating impossibly fast. The ruffled blouse fit her in a graceful way, and the short sleeves showed off her toned arms. The skirt she was wearing clung to her figure, showing off the narrow cut of her waist that flared out into powerful and womanly legs.

It was all so much, and he found himself just appreciating

the art of her more often than not. He didn't want to seem like he was leering, or somehow reducing her to just her looks, but he was caught up in everything about her. Even watching her eat her dinner made his heart beat harder.

He didn't know when he became so affected by the woman, and he hoped it wasn't creepy. But something had shifted between them when he'd picked her up off the ground during the storm, and he wasn't eager to go back to how it was before.

"So, once you save each and every animal on our evil ranch, what will you do next?"

Her eyes flew wide for barely a second before she reigned it in back into a neutral expression. He appreciated how much she schooled herself, but he also felt a swirl of pride that he was able to break through her impressive professional façade.

"I never called your ranch evil. I would like to think that I wouldn't work for an evil employer."

"Come on, if someone wrote a story about us, who would be the good guy and who would be the villain twirling his mustache?"

"Not you, I hope. You would look terrible in a mustache."

He let out a disbelieving snort. "What? Are you kidding? I'd look dashing." No, he wouldn't. He'd experimented when he was in high school and first started sporting facial hair, but the handlebar thing and the full-beard look didn't fit him. He looked good anywhere from a constant scruff to maybe an inch of growth, but that was about it.

"Uh-huh, your Ma tell you that?"

"You better believe it." He let her take another bite of her food, happy that she seemed to like it, before he tried again. "But you never answered the question."

"Oh?" She affixed him with that look that seemed to make all of his pulse points beat much harder than they should have.

"Was there a question in that beyond terrible facial hair decisions?"

"Believe it or not, the mustache was not the crux of the conversation, no." He loved her wit. She kept up with him just as much as Silas, but without the mothering his older twin always seemed to fall into.

"Huh, well I'm afraid I missed it."

He leaned forward, pushing his plate away so he could rest an arm on the table. His mother would have been appalled at his manners, but he didn't care. It was like Elizabeth was some sort of gravity well, coaxing him closer and closer with her undeniable pull.

"Once everything wraps up on the ranch, what's next for you? Do you have any dreams? Ambitions?"

"I always have ambitions."

"Well, what are they?"

She opened her mouth, but after a moment closed it again, her defined brows furrowing. "I... *oh*."

That was an interesting response. "What is it?"

"I realized that, for the first time in my life, I don't have a set goal I'm working towards."

Sterling's interest piqued at that, not that it wasn't already at one hundred percent engaged. "What do you mean?"

"Well, growing up, I dedicated my whole life to making sure I had the best scholastic record I could so I could earn enough scholarships to become a veterinarian. Literally from the age of kindergarten on, I knew exactly what I wanted to do.

"And then, once I hit college—a year early mind you—I was focusing on filling out scholarship after scholarship while trying to maintain my perfect GPA. It wasn't easy, and when my mother died, I let a few things slip."

Right, he remembered her mentioning that once. Even if he

wasn't the most affectionate person, he couldn't figure out what he would do if his mom died. She was a sweet lady, even if she was a little old-fashioned and a little too quiet when it came to standing up to their father, but he loved her.

"But I got back on track and graduated, then I was fighting to find a job. After I got a job, I was struggling to catch up on bills. Then I was fired, and now I have this job." The look on her face grew considering. "Huh, everything is pretty much caught up on. I was able to give a nice chunk of money as a gift to my dad, so he's not gonna have to worry about things so much this month. I'm even paying more than the minimum payment on my student loans, so I might actually get them taken care of in the next three years or so instead of a never-ending loop of interest.

"I've gotten pretty much everything I've been fighting for, everything I've been daydreaming about, and I don't think I realized that until just this moment." She took a deep breath, and the look she gave him was entirely open. "That's really something, isn't it?"

"Yeah, it is."

The conversation stilled for a moment, but not out of awkwardness or anything like that. Instead, it felt more like they were both digesting that revelation as well as everything that it implied.

"What about you?" Elizabeth said eventually, pulling him out of his thoughts.

"Huh?"

"Your dreams. Your ambitions. Looking for more sisters to fake-date? Or are you hoping to run into another out-of-work professional out on the main road?"

He was tempted to just joke with her, cracking wise was his

specialty, after all. But instead his mouth was shooting off on its own again, not waiting for the input from the parts of his brain that handled his pride or diplomacy.

"Being a Miller means having no ambition."

That clearly took them both by surprise. "Wow. What do you mean by that?"

Well, in for a penny, in for a pound, as it were. "It's just, uh, I guess it's—" What was it about Elizabeth that made his words go so screwy? He was the charmer, the flirt, but with her his tongue always felt like it was on a three-second delay from his mind. "My brothers and I, we're all part of an empire. We were born to be the next generation, and our purpose is whatever is decided to be the most useful for our family." He'd never put it in such plain words, but that was really how it was. "And if we're not useful, then our job is just to exist and not mess anything up. That's it." No direction. No dreams. Just to sit there on the shelf until they were useful.

Was that why he'd always felt so directionless? Was that why he'd been so willing to go along with a plan that would irritate his parents? Ruin their plans a little?

Was that why he resented Samuel? For getting away and daring to want something that he wasn't supposed to?

Was that the rift that was growing between him and both Silas and Solomon?

It hit him all at once and he found his breath picking up speed.

"That doesn't sound like a very fulfilling way to live," Elizabeth said.

"It's not," he answered, his mind spinning with the revelation. What a strange place to have it, over Italian dinners in a relatively inexpensive restaurant sitting across from an employee. It was crossing all sorts of boundaries and probably inappropriate, but he couldn't stop what was rushing through his mind. "I guess that's how this all started."

"What all started?"

"*Us.*"

"I don't understand."

"I guess I've always felt like I was in the shadow of my brother, so when I first helped you that day you were stranded on the side of the road, it was just to outdo Silas. He helped Teddy with some things, and now she and his whole family look at him like some sort of hero. Even the people at the community center seem to have accepted him when they usually frost me out.

"I realize that's a really terrible reason to help someone, but then you took over and ordered me to take you to Peggy. No one has really talked to me like that in ages, and I guess I just got swept up in all that was you."

"All that's me?"

"Yeah. You were relentless. Nothing seemed to fluster you, even when you had an unhappy, several hundred-pound pig squealing at you. In my entire life, I don't think I've ever been as driven as you were that day. And so, I just... kinda went with whatever you said."

Her eyes flicked down, and he saw the faintest flush of pink to her cheeks. "You know, most people don't describe my stubbornness like that."

"That's probably because most people are jealous of it."

"And you're not?"

Sterling smiled. "Oh no, I'm massively jealous of it. But I figure watching you might give me a chance to try to have that kind of drive myself."

She let out a heavy breath then leaned back in her seat,

crossing her arms. "Whew, when you asked me out on a date, I didn't expect a course in existentialism."

"Me either. But that seems to be where we are."

"It does." She narrowed her eyes, regarding him in that way that let him know she was thinking about what she was going to say next. "Do you feel like you've learned anything?"

"I certainly hope so. Although there is one question that remains unanswered."

"Oh really? What's that?"

He shot her what he hoped was a charming grin. "Does the Great Elizabeth Brown ever slow down?"

Her responding smile made his temperature rise several notches. "Only if I'm dead."

He whistled, but her look only grew more intense. It felt like she was staring right into the deepest parts of him, seeing all that was broken and figuring out how to fix him. Unfortunately, he wasn't like the pigpens. They couldn't buy some logs and food dispensers then declare him better.

"Have you ever been in love? Romantically?" she asked.

Whoa. That was a question out of left field if there ever was one. And yet he found himself answering anyway, caught up in the spell of the woman across from him.

"No," he said. Was that the wrong answer? It felt like it might be, but it was the truth. He'd just never felt that connection to anyone. "You?"

"No." Oh... that was... good, right? "But I feel I could be. Maybe. With someone very specific, but I'm afraid I'll never meet him. Or... what if I'm wrong?"

The rest of the restaurant could have been lit on fire and he wouldn't even know, all of his consciousness narrowed down to the beautiful, capable woman in front of him. The one who made him feel like he was fumbling along and listless, the one who made him want to be *better*.

"You know, my mom said I was in puppy love a few times when I was younger."

"Did she now?"

He nodded, wondering why he was telling something out of his embarrassing childhood. But like with so much else involving Elizabeth, he was flying by the seat of his pants. "Apparently I had two and only two puppy crushes in my young life, and that was it."

"Only two? I hear that's impressive for a teenage boy. Or at least if I'm to believe my cousins' tales of puberty."

He chuckled at that. Puberty *had* been a real weird time, with both him and his twin shooting up several inches and developing facial hair at the ripe ol' age of sixteen. Silas had definitely had the worst of it, as their sudden growth spurt had caused some of the barely healed scarring on his chest to split right back open. Actually... Sterling was pretty sure that was when his twin stopped going shirtless into pools.

"One was my Latin teacher in school, Ms. Harrington. And the other was a character from a... uh, a TV series."

"A TV series?" Elizabeth parroted, sounding quite amused. "I can tell by your pause that you're embarrassed about it, so that means you absolutely have to tell me."

"Oh really..."

"Of course. It would be terribly rude not to."

"Well heaven forbid I ever be rude." He shook his head, feeling strangely abased by the story but wanting to share it with Elizabeth anyway. He found himself wanting to split himself open and spill all of himself out to her, all the bad, the good, the lazy. He wanted her to look at what was wrong with him and give him a list that would help him feel like maybe he was around for an actual *purpose*. "It was this warrior lady type, defending her home from evil forces. Some sort of high fantasy thing on the science fiction channel. She had a sword and a spear and was just, uh, very capable."

"And in a skimpy leather outfit?"

"And in a skimpy leather outfit," he confirmed, his cheeks coloring. "But yeah, other than that, never really been drawn to anyone."

"Never?"

"Never."

She was looking at him even more intensely and if he wasn't having so much fun, he might have started to sweat. She had a gaze on her that was just so *unnerving*.

"Not even now?" she asked.

Oh.

Oooh.

His mouth opened. No words. His mouth closed. Still no words. He took a breath and tried to boot his brain back into gear, but then a loud voice spilled over him like a bucket of cold water.

"Oh hey, Silas! How are you?"

Sterling jolted and looked towards the sound to see someone approaching them. A tall man with bright red hair and a full beard. It took a few more beats before he recognized him as one of the co-owners of the small company that his brother had paid to help with renovations of the community center.

"Uh, hey," he said, standing and offering his hand. "I'm afraid—"

"You look different, buddy. You been working out? Growing out your hair?"

The man took his hand in a warm, friendly grip. Clearly, he was trying to be jovial, but it was the absolute worst timing.

"I'm sorry, sir, but there's no Silas here. But you can call me Sterling."

"Ster-what—*oh!*" He broke out into a wide grin, and Sterling got the feeling he knew why Silas had chosen the redhead's company. "You're the twin! I heard about you, but somehow, we never met before. Hi, it's good to meet you." He turned to Elizabeth and gave her a polite tip of the head. "And nice to meet the missus. You look lovely, of course."

"She's not—"

"Anyways, I better get back to my own wife. She's eight months pregnant and this might be the last time we get to eat out together before it's sleepless nights and applesauce. Good seeing you two!"

A friendly clap on his back and then the man was gone, hurrying back to the woman who was lowering herself into a seat with a hefty sigh.

"Uh, right," he said, sitting down himself. "Where were we?"

He knew exactly where they had left off, but the moment was broken. However, the question she asked played over and over again in his mind on repeat. Not because he wasn't sure of the answer, he knew that he was attracted to Elizabeth in a way he hadn't been in his entire adult life. No, the reason it kept going on repeat was because he couldn't help but wonder *why* she had asked it.

But with the interruption of the stranger, they couldn't quite slide back into the moment, and although they finished up the meal with pleasant conversation, he could never quite steer it to a place where it seemed natural that he would ask such a thing.

The conversation was still enjoyable, of course, electric even. He felt like he was getting to see a whole new side of Elizabeth, one that had been locked away before. One that most people didn't get to see.

Eventually, however, the night had long since grown dark and it was growing ever closer to the restaurant's closing time. When they were one of the last couples around, they agreed that they should go, although he certainly had plenty of hesitation on his part. He wanted to stay in the moment forever. Just the two of them, no pigs, no ranch, no money, just them.

Was this how Silas felt around Teddy? No wonder he was such a sap. And Solomon around Frenchie? Suddenly his frequent trips to visit her in the city made sense. He'd always thought they were just being ridiculous, but maybe he owed them a mental apology.

But that could wait until later. At the moment, he had Elizabeth on his arm as he walked her to her vehicle in the parking lot. He was starting to get used to not using the valet services, even if it still felt weird.

Unfortunately, they reached Elizabeth's car far too soon. She was still driving that old junker around, even if she did insist that Teddy had made the insides like new. He wasn't quite sure why she didn't just buy a new one, but he was beginning to trust that Elizabeth had a reason for why she did what she did.

"Funny, now that we're here, I kind of wish we weren't," Elizabeth said, looking up at him through her thick lashes. And if that wasn't an expression and a *half*. For someone who usually walked around the ranch with a permanent grimace on her face, she certainly knew how to make his heart pound.

Was it pathetic that he was so enthralled? Caught up in

every micromovement of her face? Probably. It couldn't be healthy.

"Me either," he said.

She let go of his arm and turned to face him. He wasn't prepared for just how close that brought them to each other, barely a hand's worth of space between them. He practically could feel the electricity of her body, the rise and fall of her chest with her breathing. It made his own exhalations pick up, his senses suddenly acutely aware of everything happening around them.

"Thank you," she said, voice soft. Low. He didn't think he had ever heard it pitched like that. "I had a lovely time."

"Good to know this pity date didn't turn out to be so bad."

"It wasn't a pity date."

She took a step forward, and Sterling swore he could feel his pulse pounding in his throat. One of her hands came to rest on his shoulder while her face tilted up to his, eyes half-lidded and expression hazy. "Definitely not a pity date," she murmured, voice barely above a whisper.

Part of his mind was in shock, because it seemed like Elizabeth was trying to kiss him. The other part of his mind was already reacting, wrapping one arm around her waist and pressing his lips to hers with perhaps less finesse than he would have liked.

But that didn't matter because the moment they kissed, everything else washed away. There was just the heat of her body, the muscles of her back strong and firm under his hand. A soft, sweet little sigh escaped her, and Sterling's head spun with the rush of it all.

Almost as soon as it started, she was stepping away. The expression she wore was a strange one, but certainly not unwelcome on her features. "Goodnight, Sterling."

"Goodnight, Elizabeth," he answered back, although his voice was noticeably shakier than hers.

And then she was getting into her car, checking to make sure Sterling was out of the way before she began pulling her junker out. Sterling watched her go, feeling like he was still lost in that kiss. Still lost in the feel of everything that was *her*.

He wasn't sure how long he stood there, but when he did eventually return to his truck, it felt like he was floating.

18

Sterling

"*Finally.*" Sterling couldn't help but sigh to himself as he finished up the last of his budget proposal to send to Silas and Solomon. Normally it was the sort of thing that he would send straight to his father, but he figured it would be prudent to have his brothers on his side considering the price tag on his plan. It went well beyond his expense account, and by went well beyond, it would be more accurate to say it was almost a total revision of how they currently handled their livestock situation.

Actually, normally Sterling wouldn't have cared about such a situation. The ins and outs of the ranch were never of much interest to him. But that had changed, along with a whole lot of other things.

As he saved the file, he realized that he understood his northern cousins a lot better. Before, when there'd been talk about the quality of life or returns on happiness of the livestock, his eyes had mostly glazed over. After all, they were a bunch of bleeding-heart hippie liberal types according to Dad. But since Elizabeth had started up with her plans, he'd already noticed a change in the pigs. They were more sociable and definitely more vocal. In only about two months, they'd had less of them chew at each other's ears or bite workers. And the contractors weren't even through half of the list.

He definitely owed his aunt and uncle an apology, too. They could go on the list of people owed one, because at the moment he wanted to head out to the pens and catch Elizabeth on her lunch break. Maybe it was sappy, but the night before, he'd packed a sort of picnic basket to share with her. He'd noticed how much she'd liked the sandwich he made her that night when he brought her home from the hospital, and if she liked that, then she'd *love* his deviled eggs.

...or at least he hoped so. It was one of four dishes he knew how to make, if only because he insisted on "helping" his mother make them for picnics so he could sneak some ahead of time.

He was only halfway to the kitchen, about to head into the main part of the house from his wing when the door that separated them burst open.

Sterling blinked, stopping in his tracks as he saw his father standing there, breathing harder than what was normal.

That was a cue that he was not around for a happy visit. And by clue, he meant a big, flashing sign. Sterling steeled himself, wondering what dark cloud had brought his father his way.

McLintoc Miller was once a solid cut of a man, a brawler who had gotten in more fights than not, fights that his older brother had often gotten him out of. But he hadn't aged gracefully, fighting the process tooth and nail. All of his sons were taller than him, wider than him, but he still made Sterling feel so small.

"Son," he said, but the term held no warmth.

"Dad," Sterling returned cautiously. Why did he feel like he was a teenager getting caught sneaking out of the house? He wasn't doing anything wrong!

"You want to tell me what's going on?"

For the first time in over a decade, there were too many possible answers. Sterling was so used to doing nothing, but between his soil tests, the pens, and his proposal to expand Elizabeth's expertise to the rest of the ranch, he had a lot of projects that he was juggling. A lot of very *expensive* projects.

"Sir?" he said instead when it was very clear that his father wanted an answer.

"I was just talking with my good friend Colunius—"

Who named their kid Colunius, even in the sixties?

"—and he said that his son spotted you out with a woman at a restaurant in the city."

"...I am allowed to go out, Dad, last time I checked."

McLintoc Miller rolled his eyes. "Why are all of you so dramatic? No one is saying that. I just want to know what possible reason you could have for being out with someone like... *her*."

It was like someone poured ice-cold water down his back. "What do you mean?"

"You know what I mean."

"No, I'm afraid I don't."

That, apparently, was the wrong thing to say, because Mr. Miller's face went red as a beet and he raised his cane, slamming it against the wall with a resounding *thwack*. Sterling flinched on instinct, even though his father hadn't raised a hand to him since that day he'd gotten his brother permanently disfigured for life with a single firecracker.

"Tell me since when do you keep company with some lower-class black woman? Huh? You know what that looks like for us?"

"Elizabeth isn't—"

"*Elizabeth*!? So she has a name now?"

"Yeah, Dad. People have names, don't you know?"

Another smack and this time Sterling squared his shoulders. It was one thing when his dad set in on him or his family, but it was another to insult Elizabeth. It went against every nerve in Sterling's body and he found himself wanting to protect the woman, even if she had no idea what his father was saying.

"Where did I go wrong? How is it that half of my sons are running around with street trash? Do you want to ruin our reputation, or are you all so stupid that none of you can recognize gold diggers when they bite you right in the face!?"

Some small, young part of Sterling wanted to curl up, to apologize and do whatever he needed to please his father. To show off for him, to prove that he was a *good* son, a son that he could be proud of. But the bigger part of him roared at the disrespect of the woman he was falling in love with.

Elizabeth was smart, intense, strong, capable. She had a heart as big as their entire estate, even if she usually only let animals into it. She was hard-working. She was determined. And she deserved so much better than some rich, wrinkly old man besmirching her character.

"Elizabeth isn't a gold digger," Sterling said as calmly as he could, which turned out to not be very calm at all. "She's a veterinarian and an amazing woman."

"Oh yeah, I'm sure. Have you seen her degree? And just

how did you meet this supposed 'veterinarian'? Was she a streetwalker like Solomon's"—his nose wrinkled, and Sterling's temper jumped up that much hotter—"*plaything?*"

"Frenchie was *not* a prostitute," Sterling snapped, taking a step closer to his father. "And even if she *were*, she isn't now. She is *engaged* to your son and set to be your daughter-in-law."

"Not if I have anything to say about it."

His temper jumped up again. Sterling couldn't remember a time when he'd been so angry. He hadn't had something he really cared about enough to get angry over. "You don't, Dad."

"What?"

He kept on. He didn't know where his strength was coming from, but he wasn't going to stand there and let his own father speak ill of the world that Sterling was just discovering. "You don't get to say anything about it, Dad. We're your sons, yes, but you don't get to dictate our destinies because of that. We're going to date who we want to date, fall in love with who we want to fall in love with. We're going to open the community centers we want to; fund the charities we want to. And when you're old and decrepit, we're going to run this ranch the way we want to.

"I know it makes you angry that you can't be in charge forever, and that we're proving to be our own people. Feels like sand running out of your hands, right?" He took one last step towards his father, bringing them face-to-face. He felt like he'd always known what had brought on his dad's sourness, his meanness, his nit-picking, but it was the first time he'd ever admitted it to himself. Because speaking it meant that he couldn't pretend his dad was a good guy anymore. And if his father wasn't a good man, then neither were any of them as long as they let him dictate their life.

"But here's the thing, Dad. You're going to keep getting

older, and soon you'll have to rely on us. Do you really want to turn all of us into your enemy? Because, even though I'm sure you'd like to deny it, you're still human. And humans get old. We die. You can't run things forever."

His father was practically shaking with rage by the time Sterling finished, but the younger twin wasn't scared. "I will write you out of the will. You ungrateful little brat."

"Do it. I'm sure Mom will be real thrilled that you've cut off two of her sons in as many years. And if Samuel is doing just fine without you, I think I'll be just fine too."

"That gold digger of yours will leave you and then you'll be the fool. When you come crawling back to me, I won't let you back in."

"Oh, Dad," Sterling let his tone soften, stepping around his father. "Elizabeth isn't mine to lose. But maybe, if I play my cards right, she could be."

Sterling didn't break his stride, traveling into the main house and heading for the kitchen. He heard his father sputtering after him, spitting curses that the good Lord wouldn't approve of, but Sterling ignored him.

Yes, he owed his father a certain kind of respect, but in order for that to happen, his father had to treat them with respect as well. He didn't get to insult Frenchie or Teddy or Elizabeth. He didn't get to assume things about their character just because they weren't born into money.

Because—although he would never admit it—their father had been born into wealth the same way Sterling and his brothers had been. And so had his father's father. And his father's father's father. The Miller line had been wealthy for so many generations that no one could remember a time where money had ever been a worry for them. Without that kind of backing, McLintoc Miller wouldn't be who he was.

Grabbing the picnic basket he'd set in their second fridge in the pantry room, he headed out to his truck. Although he was too far from his father to actually catch any words, he swore he still heard the man in his head, all red-faced and spitting nails. Sterling was glad that he had stood up to the man, but he still felt affected. His heart was pounding, his palms were sweaty, and he was stuck somewhere between upset, angry and hurt. Standing up to his father had drawn a line in the sand, and he didn't entirely know what the consequences would be of establishing that boundary.

But there were to be consequences, that much he was sure of.

It didn't take long for him to arrive at the pens, catching Elizabeth just as she exited from the interior doors of the barn. He took a deep breath, trying to shove his swirling emotions down so they could enjoy the picnic he'd planned, but then he was caught up in those eyes of hers and it was clear that she instantly saw through him.

"What's wrong?" she asked, her brows furrowing together.

"I... it's nothing. You don't need to know." Truth was that Sterling couldn't bring himself to repeat what his father had said. If only because it would confirm everything that she had confessed she suspected of his family.

And also, because he was embarrassed. He couldn't control what his father said, but he still felt ashamed about it.

But her hand was gentle on his shoulder. "I can tell it's not nothing. You don't have to tell me if it's private, but you also don't have to *not* tell me. I'm a good listener."

He was tempted, because of course he was. He'd long since learned that he had a difficult time saying no to anything the woman asked, even if it did make his cheeks color with embarrassment.

Yet before he could speak, his phone was ringing shrilly. Elizabeth's eyebrows raised, and he held up a finger to hold the conversation. Just like when they had first met, his phone only rang in emergencies.

"It's Silas," he said once he checked his phone screen, quickly sliding his finger to accept the call. "What's—"

"Get the vet and bring her to the middle of our racing trail!" his brother blurted out, cutting off his greeting.

"Wait, what?"

"My horse is hurt, get her here, okay?"

"Of course. She's right in front of me. You said in the middle?"

"Yeah."

Elizabeth must have had impeccable hearing because she held her hand out for the phone. And just like before, Sterling handed it to her.

"Tell me what's going on," she said with authority as they both jogged to his truck.

Sterling tuned them out, concentrating on driving as quickly as he could.

It wasn't easy to get to the middle of their racing trail. That was the whole reason it was where it was, set apart from the rest of the estate and the regularly traveled paths.

When they finally did arrive, he had to slow down. The last thing he wanted was to accidentally run over his brother or his horse. That would most certainly be the opposite outcome that they wanted.

"There!" Elizabeth said, pointing ahead and just to the right to the track he and his twin had beaten into the ground.

Sure enough, Silas was kneeling off to the side, his pretty mount next to him, breathing harshly.

Sterling skidded to a stop, and Elizabeth practically vaulted out of the passenger's side. He threw the truck into park and followed her, his heart squeezing in his chest.

Although he would never admit it, Sterling had become fairly attached to his own mount, and Silas was *much* closer with his horse. He couldn't imagine what was going through his twin's mind.

Except he could. That connection they shared burned hot and bright in his mind, making his stomach twist tightly.

"She got her hoof in a gopher hole," Silas said, panic layering his voice. "She's really hurt her leg."

"It's alright. Let me feel it out. Is she a kicker?"

"Not generally, but she's in pain. I'm... I'm worried it's broken. Or irreparably damaged. That's what happens to a horse, right? When they're hurt?"

Elizabeth reached over and squeezed his twin's hand, surprising Sterling. She wasn't the most tactile of people. "Don't worry. Even if there's damage, there's no reason she can't live a full and healthy life."

"Really? Okay. That's good. That's really good."

"Now, if you don't mind giving me some space, let me calm her down and tell her it's gonna be alright?"

"You can do that?"

"I can certainly try."

She knelt in the same spot Silas had just been, her hands gently sliding through the horse's carefully kept mane. Sterling gave the whole scene a wide berth, circling around until he was next to his twin. Offering his hand, he pulled him up into a hug.

"It's okay," he said with as much certainty as he could muster. "She's gonna take care of her. I promise."

Silas nodded, his mouth a thin line, but he didn't pull out of the hug. Sterling couldn't remember the last time that they had embraced. High school, maybe? When had so much distance come between them?

"Hey there, beautiful. I hear you've had a pretty crappy morning," Elizabeth murmured, voice low and soothing, like a blanket. Her hands continued to move along the horse, scratching all those spaces that horses tended to like to be petted. "I'm going to need to look at your leg, okay? I might even make it go owie, but I promise I'm just trying to make you better. Okay?"

The horse waffled and if Sterling didn't know better, he would think that the creature understood her.

Elizabeth continued, "That's my girl. You're so brave, you know that? Such a brave girl."

Slowly, slowly, Elizabeth moved her hands down the horse's body, scratching her spine, rubbing her flanks. Bit by bit she moved, until she was parallel to the front leg that was already swollen.

"Hey, Silas, I want you to come stand right behind me so she knows you approve of this. Sterling, can you hold and pet her head?"

The twins separated and went to do as she said. Sterling didn't know why it wasn't better for Silas to hold the horse's head, but he knew better than to question Elizabeth's instructions. She was the one with the degree, after all.

So that was how he found the ride's head in his lap, petting and comforting her as best he knew how. He certainly was no Elizabeth, but he figured he was better than nothing.

The horse, for her hard breathing and panting, was surprisingly calm. She whinnied once when Elizabeth put pressure on where she was hurt but didn't try to kick. Didn't chomp. Her gaze mostly stayed on the two in front of her, but every now and then her big, beautiful eyes would flick up to the human who was petting her mane.

Sterling hadn't expected to see much besides his own reflection, but *wow*, was he wrong. There was so much in the animal's stare, and he couldn't help but be surprised by it. There was intelligence there, and fear. A need for assurance, a worried sort of uncertainty. It made his already hurting heart ache for her.

And it was probably in that moment that something clicked within him, and he understood Elizabeth even more than before. A strange flare of emotion rose within him, thinking that for many of their animals on the ranch, she was the only bright spot in their lives. The only person who treated them like *beings* instead of objects. Instead of profits.

Oh.

Sure, he respected Elizabeth's opinions enough to want to implement them to more of their ranch, but he hadn't really *understood* it. Until right then and there, with the horse's head in his lap, looking at him like she was terrified of what could be.

Wow. His family had a whole lot to make up for.

Time slipped by as she inspected, then made some calls to the other vets they had on contract. Sterling only half-listened as she set up the details, then as she assured his brother that his mount would be okay. His eyes were locked onto the horses, wondering just how many sad, sad animals populated their property.

Eventually, however, a horse trailer came to pick up the mount, and transport was arranged to her stall. Apparently, the girl wouldn't need a ride to the surgery center in the city, but definitely would need a long, *long* recovery to let it heal.

When all was said and done, Sterling drove Elizabeth back

to the pens. It felt like his mind was only just catching up with everything that had happened. From his personal revelations, to how effortlessly Elizabeth handled the situation. How sure and kind she was with the very scared and injured animal. What his father had assumed about her. It was all so much, and yet one thing shone sharp and bright in his mind. *One* thing had certainty to it.

He waited until he was walking her to her car, knowing that she wanted to drive to the stables and tend to the horse well past the hours that she was supposed to work. But before she got in, his mouth was doing that thing where it ran off on its own again.

"Hey," he said suddenly as she opened her car door, clearly startling her.

She jumped, holding a hand to her heart. "Goodness, if you scared me just to tell me a horse joke right now, I might run over you."

That was his girl. Well, not his girl *yet*, actually. "I'm pretty sure I would deserve it."

"You would." She leveled him with one of her serious looks. "Were you gonna say something?"

"Yes. I was." When he didn't immediately speak again, she raised one of her eyebrows in that way that only she did. He knew he had seconds before he chickened out, so he decided to just go in on the runaway mouth thing full force. "You want to go steady?"

She blinked at him and then a short, dry sort of chuckle escaped her mouth. "No one calls it that anymore."

"Well, I am. Right now."

She gave him a long look, one of those that stared through his soul. "It's a bit soon, to be honest."

Oh no.

Oh *no*.

His heart felt like someone had shot an arrow through it, ripping it out of his body and pinning it somewhere hard and cold. But before he had to scramble an apology for even asking her, she was speaking again.

"But, if we have a couple more dates that go well, I think I'm game to try."

It was like the whole world had been plunged into darkness only to be catapulted into daylight. "You think?"

She winked at him, actually *winked*, and it was such a not-Elizabeth thing that he almost wondered if he had imagined it. "Well, I wouldn't want to jinx it."

"Hold on," he said.

Sterling ran to his truck, grabbed the picnic basket, and put it in her car. "You'll get hungry. Might as well not let this go to waste."

Elizabeth smiled, eyes wide. "Thank you."

And then she was sliding into her car and driving off, leaving Sterling with a "couple more" dates to plan.

He was very much up to the challenge.

19

Elizabeth

"*D*o you think there's an after-credits scene here?" Sterling said, his warm breath brushing against her ear. Goosebumps rose along Elizabeth's skin, her body reacting viscerally to Sterling just like it always did.

She wanted to say that she hated it, but she didn't. Ever since that date at the restaurant, it felt like her every sense had been ramped up to one hundred every time that Sterling came around.

And he was coming around a *whole* lot.

They tended to have lunch together every day that they worked, and she couldn't believe it that he specially packed them a picnic basket every time. It was thoughtful, even if it seemed like he could only make about four things. Although, in the month and a half since he had asked her out, he seemed to have picked up two new recipes, judging by the quesadillas and biscuits he made—with varied success.

It was strange to think of how much had changed in that month and a half, or in the almost four since she had taken the job. The pigpens were shaping up more than ever, but when she went on to explore the other livestock just so she could get ahead and take her time planning, she was almost overwhelmed with all the work that needed to be done.

So, in a way, it was much harder, but in other ways, it was *so* much easier.

Almost every other afternoon was spent with Mrs. Miller in her gardens or chicken coop, which Frenchie and Teddy apparently also spent plenty of time in. The four of them ended up building a strange sort of bond, three poor girls and a rich white lady. It was unorthodox, sure, but sincere. Elizabeth got the feeling that Mrs. Miller was lonely, considering how much of her time she spent surrounded by men.

"No one does after-the-credits scenes since those superhero movies ended."

"Those superhero movies?" Sterling whispered back in amusement. "Are you calling some of the most blockbuster movies of this decade *those* superhero movies?"

"Since when do cowboys watch comic book movies?"

"Since when am I a cowboy?"

"You live on a ranch. You ride horses. Close enough."

He chuckled, and the sound made goosebumps rise along her arms. He truly had no idea how much he affected her.

Which was good, because if he did know... well, it would be embarrassing, that was for certain. Elizabeth had always been the calm and collected girl, the type of person whose nose was too busy against the grindstone to care anything about romance or crushes. But when she looked at Sterling, well, a lot of that flew right out the window.

It didn't hurt that he was stunningly handsome, but it was so much more than that. Sure, in the month and a half that they had been casually dating, he still said some stuff that made her give him the side-eye, but she could tell that he was trying, and that's what meant so much to her.

He never told her she was odd, never told her she was wrong, he never even told her that she cared for animals too much. No, according to what Sterling said, she was practically perfect. Which of course wasn't true, but goodness, it sure did make her feel special.

Elizabeth spent so much of her life being not understood. At being an "other." At being that strange girl who was practically inhuman. Her mother had loved her, of course. Her father loved her. But she'd never really had friends, never really had anyone she was that close to. Sure, she had other nerds that she formed bonds with. Safety in numbers, after all. And they had goaded each other with friendly competitions and challenges. But she'd never felt connected to someone like she had become connected to Sterling in the past few weeks. She hadn't even known it was possible.

And she certainly hadn't thought it would be with a billionaire whose family had a history of standing for things that had hurt folks like her. Honestly, if Sterling was anything like his father, it would have ended things point-blank. But the closer they became, the more he confided in her, the more she believed that he wanted to undo all the things their empire had done to hurt others. Starting with their workers and their animals.

"Well, if there's no after-credits scene, do you wanna head out?"

She didn't. Not really. She wanted to stay in the dark theater, her fingers intertwined through Sterling's. Tucked away from the rest of the world. Just him and her and the words rolling up the screen. But her bladder gave a protesting pang, so she let out a sigh.

"Yeah, that's probably for the best."

They headed out of the theater hand in hand, following the gentle flow of traffic. Once in the lobby, they parted so Elizabeth could take care of her business, and when she returned, he was waiting at the door for her.

"Ready?" he asked.

She nodded, taking his arm as they always did lately, and let him lead her outside.

They had parked all the way at the opposite end of the lot. It was nearing the end of summer and the night had cooled off, with a lovely breeze. It was the perfect weather to stroll along casually, looking up at the night sky.

"Hey," she said, leaning her head against his strong arm. "Want to take a couple laps?"

"Sure. There's not much traffic. We'll just make sure to avoid the exit and entrance."

"Nah, let's just do the Macarena right in front of them."

"You know, I might just die of embarrassment if you make me do that," he said, smiling that crooked, charming smile at her. The one that made her knees weak if she didn't think carefully about tightening her muscles.

"Well, you're in luck then because I've never actually danced the Macarena before."

"That's alright, we can be bad at it together."

He made her laugh. Goodness, was he good at making her laugh. And she knew it was crazy, but she could really see a future with him, growing together, learning. She liked that he brought a side out of herself that she wasn't used to. Someone a bit more social, someone a little less tightly wound. Sure, she still terrified half of the workers, but as she had said before, their bloodlines were weak. She had more friends than she had ever had before and that was all because of him.

"You know, nights like this make me dread when winter finally shows up," Sterling said after a while, gently squeezing her arm.

"You mean when it gets down in the fifties and we laugh at the people up north who are freezing their tushies off?"

"Well, I don't know about *laughing*, but I'll admit there might be some level of *schadenfreude*."

"Oooh, '*schadenfreude*'? Someone's been looking up five-dollar words."

"It means—"

"I know what it means," Elizabeth said quickly. "I had access to the internet when a certain play made that word popular. You know, back when I was a teenager and working a fast-food job, lost in the feeling of *Weltschmerz*." She didn't know what inspired her, maybe it was more of that sauciness that Sterling drew out of her. "But you know, being with you is definitely more along the lines of *Gemütlichkeit,* I think."

"Wait, I think I know that one, smarty-pants." Sterling wrinkled his brow.

Goodness if he didn't look fetching when he was puzzling something out. Then again, when didn't he look fetching? Sometimes Elizabeth felt like she could stare and stare at his face and never drink her fill. What *had* he done to her?

"Isn't it something about being cozy?" he said.

"Close," she said, her heart filling with warmth.

What a strange reaction to him knowing a bit of trivia. But in the month and the half of their casual dating, she had learned that her heart did whatever it wanted to do, and she was no more able to stop it than most people were able to stop her when she put her mind to something.

She continued, "It's more than that, though. It's the feeling of being on a warm, comfy couch, snuggled under a blanket with someone you love. It's about feeling truly comfortable, safe and protected. It's a single word that stands for everything that makes you feel good and fuzzy and cherished. Amazing how the Germans just condense it, isn't it?"

She was all ready to launch into a discussion of Germanic linguistics and their integration with the Latin lexicon when she realized Sterling had stopped in his tracks, the tension of her arm tugging her to a stop. Turning, she saw that he looked rather dumbfounded, seriousness swirling in that gaze of his.

"And I make you feel like that?" he asked.

His voice had dropped low again, like it did whenever they were being romantic, or they were about to kiss. It never failed to make her heart pick up in her chest, and she licked her lips on instinct.

"Well... yeah. You do."

He pulled her closer to him. She didn't think she would *ever* get over how his strong, muscled outline felt near her own feminine form. It made her skin heat, made her want to get closer to him until they were the same person, but she usually was able to shove those temptations down.

Usually, but how he was looking at her just wasn't *fair*.

She was so caught up in his expression that she didn't notice his hand coming up to cup her chin, tilting it to look right up into those startling, handsome eyes of his. "Are you joshing me?"

"No one says joshing anymore," she said, feeling her eyelids flutter. She was going all foggy-headed and distracted, as she usually did whenever their faces were so close. If only the folks from her major could see her now. Stone-hearted Lizzy enamored with a cowboy who was too handsome for her own good.

"*Elizabeth*," he murmured, voice lower, more urgent. "I know you like to play word games, but I need to know, because every day I feel like I'm falling deeper and deeper for you, but I don't have a clue how you're doing on your side. Am I making a fool of myself here?"

She knew what he was asking, and yet somehow it had surprised her. She'd said she needed time, a couple more good dates. In her opinion, they'd gone well beyond that, and she had anticipated that the eager man would ask her again. When he hadn't, she'd thought that maybe *he'd* thought better of it and wanted more time himself.

But what he was saying made it sound like he *was* waiting for her to say it was time, and she could only chuckle slightly at their silly misunderstanding.

"What's so funny?" he asked, narrowing his eyes slightly, his tone ticking towards humorous. "You are joshing me, ain't ya?"

"I'm just waiting for you to ask me again."

That didn't seem to be the answer he was expecting, and he cocked his head to the side. "Ask you what again…"

"You asked me to go steady, and I said that I needed more time. A couple good dates. Well, we've definitely had more of that. I don't know about you, but I'm *definitely* enjoying your company, so I was just waiting for you to ask me again."

"So you could say yes?" he said slowly as if he couldn't quite believe what he was hearing.

Elizabeth didn't blame him; she probably *could* have communicated the whole thing better. Oh well, she could work on that. Because she was beginning to understand that she wasn't some strange pariah. Not a woman whose brain worked differently than every other human. Sure, she wasn't exactly *normal*, or *neurotypical*, as her mother would have said. But she wasn't an alien either. Sterling got her, and so did her new friends.

"So, I can say yes," she affirmed gently.

Sterling took a deep breath, and she could practically feel his heart beating against her. "Elizabeth, I've enjoyed dating you, and I'd be right happy if you decided that I might be something along the terms of boyfriend material."

"Boyfriend material, huh?" she asked, tipping her head back like he did and allowing herself a laugh. "I think you might be a whole boyfriend quilt."

"Is that a compliment?" he shot right back, his eyes shining as they regarded her.

She didn't know how there could be starlight reflected in them, considering he was looking *down* at her, but that was exactly what she saw.

"It is if I say it is."

"Alright then, I trust you."

"I trust you too, you're my boyfriend after all."

Those words seemed to trigger something in him, his cheeks flushing pink. At that, one of his hands went to her waist, and his head bent down so that his lips could claim hers.

It was the perfect kiss, just like the rest of their kisses were perfect, full of heat and affection and kindness that she wasn't used to. It made her float, it made her head spin, and it made everything else in the world fall away.

It lasted longer than their normal kisses, one of his palms on her waist and the other still resting warm across her chin. Sometimes she felt like the way he held her was the only thing that kept her tethered to earth.

But then, like usual, he was the one who broke the kiss with her leaning after him almost dazedly. But unlike usual, she barely had time to blink before he was picking her up and spinning her around.

"Ah! Sterling! You set me down!" she cried through her laughter, looking up at the night sky as the stars twirled and twirled over her head. "I am tall enough already! I do not need to be this high off the ground!"

He spun around a couple more times before setting her down. She nearly collapsed against his chest, breathing raggedly.

"You're lucky I like you," she said with chagrin as she caught her breath.

"And don't I know it," he said without a lick of sarcasm.

Oh. Her cheeks flushed red at that. How was he able to so unabashedly compliment her like that? Just state that she was important to him without any hesitation? It never failed to make her react. And she treasured every single one of those moments, vowing to herself that she would find some way to make Sterling feel as special as he made her feel.

"Would you like to visit the cats that have taken up in one of the garages? Teddy just told Silas about them. Apparently, there's a calico with multiple toes and she's a beauty."

"He."

"Huh?"

Elizabeth grinned, feeling so very in love. "All calico cats are females because it's a recessive trait that's carried on the X gene."

"So then... she would be a she, right?"

"Would be, if not for the extra toes. Male calicos are very rare, due to an XXY mutation. They're sterile, and they have extra toes. They're incredibly valuable, not that I care about that last part."

Sterling shook his head, chuckling at her and offering her his arm again. "You always are something, Elizabeth. But please, tell me more cat facts on the drive back home."

"Are you sure? It's a pretty long ride. What if I run out?"

Sterling gave her a rueful look. "When pigs fly."

"Well, maybe, but there's a lot of work left to be done to figure out *that* particular genetic sequence."

"If anyone could do it, it's you. You're the smartest woman I've ever met."

Geez. Cheeks practically on fire, Elizabeth hopped up into his truck. She wasn't used to being outmaneuvered by someone, but clearly Sterling was beating her hand over fist in the casual compliments' territory.

That's alright. She had always been an excellent study.

20

Elizabeth

The intercom buzzed and Elizabeth jumped nearly a foot into the air. *Yikes!* She was going to have to get used to that or she was gonna die very early of an apoplexy.

"Coming!" she called out of habit before remembering that whoever was on the other side wouldn't be able to hear her. Right, she knew how intercoms worked. She was just excited and exhausted and excited and...

It buzzed again and she jumped just as much the second time. Hurrying over, she pressed the button that let her talk to whoever was at the door.

"Somebody is mighty impatient," she said, perhaps over-enunciating her words a bit.

"Well, I guess *somebody* is just excited to see their girl-friend's new place."

Elizabeth felt herself flush at that. Silly, she was thirty years old and still getting heart palpitations after six months of being a couple.

It hadn't been an easy six months, and yet it also had. Winter had come and mostly gone, the pigpens were practically done, and she was kinda-sorta working on upgrading the breeding area for the cows. The "kinda-sorta" part came in because Sterling and his two brothers appeared to be in the middle of a multi-month battle with their father, trying to get him to agree on allocating a significant amount of budget for making the ranch more animal-friendly.

Apparently, the patriarch of the household gave the same blowback that most people gave Elizabeth. The creatures were meant to be eaten; what was the point in spending all that money on their enrichment? That was always the issue when people tended to value money over life. Yes, man was given dominion over animals by God, but that meant caring for and respecting them, *especially* if they were going to be giving up their lives to sustain others.

Thankfully, that wasn't a fight she had to take part in, mostly she just had to support Sterling from the side and listen to him vent. Which she was more than happy to do. Sometimes her father would tag in as well, and ever since the winter had waned, the two men had been going on Saturday fishing trips about once a month.

It was so good to see her father socializing again, even though it may have been weird that it was with her boyfriend. Except she didn't find it weird at all. She felt like if anyone could use a kind and understanding father figure, it was Sterling, and maybe her dad sensed that.

"Well, are you gonna buzz me in or what?"

Elizabeth blinked. It wasn't like her to drift so much, but

after working all weekend to move, she was perhaps a bit distracted. "I pressed the button; didn't it work?"

"...very obviously not, sweetheart."

Ugh. It wasn't fair how he could say a single word such as sweetheart and have her blood rushing in her ears. Swallowing, she shook her head. *Later.* "Alright, let me try another one."

She did so, and there was a corresponding loud beep from below.

"There you are. Be up in a jiffy. Second floor you said, right?"

"Righto."

His voice cut off, and then she heard the outer door buzz again and quick footsteps up the singular flight of stairs to her place.

Another way life had gotten both easier and harder was that after over six months of steady and frankly amazing pay, she'd caught up on all of her bills and then some, paid ahead on her loan and had finally found a new place.

Gone was her tiny, studio apartment that she rented over a bar in a small town an hour and fifty minutes from the city. Instead, she had a lovely one-bedroom apartment on the edge of the city limits that was about three times as big. And—more importantly—allowed cats.

A knock sounded at her door and she practically threw it open, revealing Sterling standing there with a bouquet of flowers in his hand. He still looked as handsome as ever, eyes sparkling with excitement as he looked past her.

"So, is there a tour of this place or was I supposed to sign up somewhere?"

"I dunno," Elizabeth retorted, leaning on the door like she was considering not letting him in. "This place will probably look real crummy compared to your tastes."

"Nah, if you picked it, I trust your taste. Besides, out of the two of us, who do you think is better at balancing a budget?"

"Fair enough," she said, laughing at the same time that she blushed. "Alright, this way!"

She excitedly showed him her kitchen, the dining room, then the living room. It was so nice to have separate spaces for all of those things, since previously her whole home had been one room.

Then she went on to the bathroom, which had just about *the* nicest tub of any home she'd ever had. Sterling didn't seem to get why that was such a big deal to her, but he nodded and smiled nonetheless and that was enough.

The bedroom was only a quick flash, her pointing out the nice reading nook she had with one of the larger windows and then quickly shutting the door. It wasn't that she was embarrassed. Not at all. But having the man that she was intensely attracted to and definitely in love with standing in the same space as her bed led to far too much temptation. After all, she was only human. Besides, she'd just gotten her life back on track. There was no reason to derail it by biting into that particular apple, so to speak.

Even if it was the yummiest, prettiest apple that she had *ever* seen.

"Hey, you alright there?"

Elizabeth nodded, hurrying back to the living room. "So yeah, that's my new place!" she said, making a broad gesture.

"Well, I wish you would have let me and my brothers help you move, but it looks mighty nice."

She shrugged. "You all had a conference you needed to attend, and this was something that I wanted to do on my own. I mean, Dad helped, and I paid some guys for the real heavy lifting, but this was a fun project."

He shook his head, closing the distance between them to gently rest his hands at her waist. "Only you would think that moving yourself in and decorating entirely on your own was a fun project."

She shrugged. "Better than it being a trial, right?"

He smiled, bending down to press a kiss to her forehead. It was such a simple thing, and yet it made her feel safe. Secure. Like nothing could touch her as long as she had him at her side.

"I can't argue with that logic there."

"Good, because you'd lose."

He raised his eyebrow but chuckled instead of arguing further. "Once, not even Silas could claim that. But you? I guess you really are one of a kind."

"Careful," she said, stepping back and fanning her face. "You know what we said about compliment flooding."

"It's not *my* fault that I just want to point out all the things I like about you."

She rolled her eyes, because sometimes it was the only defense that she had against the way her heart rushed when he really got going. "You'd think you'd run out eventually."

"Never."

Both of her hands went to her cheeks and she shook her head. "Alright, I give in. You're too smooth for me. Please, have mercy on a poor, flustered soul."

"I dunno," he said, dipping his head down to kiss the back of her hands. "I kinda like that I'm the only one who seems to be able to give the terrifying Elizabeth Brown pause."

"Pfft, you've been hanging around your workers too much."

"The contractors, actually. The workers are mostly sure that you won't turn them to stone on sight... mostly."

"Well. I'll have to make sure to scare them all over again.

Can't have them thinking I'm getting soft just because I'm dating their boss."

"I'm pretty sure none of them think that."

"*Good.*"

He laughed again, that loose, happy sound that she still wasn't tired of. She didn't think it was physically possible.

"You know, it's moments like these where I can *kinda* see why they're still wary of you more than half a year later," he said.

"Hey, I worked hard to establish my cold and direct persona. It would be terrible to lose all of that in less than a year."

"Yeah, yeah." His tone softened and his eyes had that *look* that he got whenever he was going to say something that made her heart thunder. "You know, I'm proud of you. You've taken what was supposed to be a fairly straightforward contract and pushed it to get results I never dreamed of."

He gently traced one of her baby hairs, his touch so gentle, so *kind*. He made her want to be better. Despite all their joking, he made her want to open up and maybe be *slightly* less brusque when she was working. She never, ever intended to be mean, but a little bit of levity slipped into her professional demeanor certainly didn't hurt.

He continued, "And I know your mom and dad are just as proud, even if one of them is watching at a distance."

Tears pricked at the corner of her eyes. "You think so?"

"I know so."

"Dad spill the beans on your last fishing trip?" she teased.

"Nah, I just know. Speaking of which..." He leaned back from her again, just enough to look down at her face. "Do you wanna go pick him up so he can see the full place now that it's finished?"

She brightened. Since having her job with Sterling, she'd been able to afford to see her dad more often too. The wonders of being able to afford gas and also not pick up secondary gigs to try to save up. Instead of seeing him once every other month or so, she managed about every other week instead.

"Yeah, that's a great idea."

Hand in hand, they headed down the stairs. But not before she punched in the code to lock her door. She *loved* that she had keyless exit and entry, for when she was running behind, or her keys were covered in farm muck. Although most of her time was spent inspecting and researching improvements, she still spent plenty of time getting in the mud or dirt and checking on the animals' health.

But when she got to her assigned parking spot in the small lot, her car wasn't there. Not only was her car *not* there, but there was someone else's parked right where it was supposed to be.

"Wait a minute," she said, dropping Sterling's hand and looking around. Was she so exhausted by working that she had accidentally parked somewhere else? She was pretty sure that she remembered pulling up into space number nineteen.

"What's wrong?" Sterling asked.

"My car. It's supposed to be there."

"Are you sure you didn't park somewhere else?"

"I'm pretty sure that I didn't. And even if I did, someone shouldn't be parked in my designated spot. They're assigned per apartment."

"Hmm. Looks like there's a piece of paper taped to the inside of the window. Maybe there's a clue whose it is? Then you can go to the office and ask them to call whoever owns it."

"Right. I guess." She didn't like the idea of using the office to solve something her first week in her new place, but she couldn't very well go knocking door-to-door.

She crossed to the front of the car and pulled out her phone, intending to take a picture of the piece of paper that might identify the owner. But when her eyes landed on it, she froze right where she was.

"What's going on?" Sterling asked from behind her.

His tone was... *off*, but she couldn't place it, mostly because her entire brain seemed to be focused on puzzling out why it was *her* name on the car title in front of her.

"I—what? There's—" she shook her head, clearing her cluttered thoughts. "My name is on this car."

"Really?" Sterling said, still in that strange tone. "You sure about that?"

"I know my own name. Why—" Oh. She finally caught onto his strange tone and turned, seeing a broad smile break across his face. "You did this," she accused, pointing a finger at him.

"I will only admit to that if you like it," he said, taking her hand in his. "I just wanted to do something special. A gift that could maybe show at least a little of how much you mean to me. And I know that you could have gotten this on your own. Remember when you were shopping around on your phone at lunch? You already had your budget figured out and a payment plan, and I realized that this was at least one thing I could do to pay you back for everything you've done for me."

"I-I..." She didn't know what to say. He had bought her a *car*. And not because he didn't think she *couldn't* and that he needed to sweep in and save her, but because he wanted to be kind.

There was a time, not even that long ago, where she wouldn't have believed him. Where she would have accused him of thinking he was better than her, of patronizing her.

Where she would have shoved him back and declared that she could take care of *herself*. After all, her mother had always said she was so independent that she wouldn't just look a gift horse in the mouth, she would give it a full veterinary checkup then declare she was buying it herself.

But she'd grown. Sure, she had no shame in being direct, in being in charge, but she also learned that sometimes, people just wanted to help people to be kind. And that it wasn't a show of *weakness* to take that help. She could accept a gift and still be the strong, capable Elizabeth that she'd always been.

As long as no one called her Lizzy, of course.

"Thank you," she said, closing the space between him again and standing up on her toes to pepper kisses all over his face. That strong nose of his, the slight dimple at the end of his chin. His cheeks, his forehead, everywhere she could reach. She just felt *so* much for the man in front of her. And not just because he bought her things, but because he *cared*.

"Whew, I'm glad you took that well because that's kind of not all."

"Hmm?" she asked, pulling back. She knew that he'd said something, but she'd been too busy showering him in her affection to listen quite as well as she should have.

"Here are the keys," he said, pulling them out of his pocket. "Check the glove compartment."

Cautiously, she did so, wondering what could be happening. What, was there a puppy waiting in there or something? No, he wouldn't do that, if only because she'd probably lectured him and every one of his family that would listen about leaving pets unattended in vehicles without proper air filtration.

Looking back to him repeatedly for some type of clue—which he gave *none*, the self-assured cowboy—she unlocked the car and bent forward. She was pleased to see that all of her stuff was already in place, from her aux cord and phone charger to the baggie of papers that she always had in her glove compartment.

But on top of that very stuffed sandwich baggy was a card, shining silver and bright. Carefully, she grasped it and stepped back out of the car so she could straighten.

"What is it?" she asked, feeling more nervous than she should have considering it was just a piece of paper in her hands.

A really *pretty* piece of paper.

"Looks like a card," Sterling said.

"I know that. But what *is* it?"

"I dunno, but I hear that reading them can be really helpful." She gave him one of her *looks,* but he just shrugged. "I think I've built up a bit of an immunity to those looks."

"That's what you think," she grumbled before opening it with trembling hands.

It was empty of any pre-written message inside, leaving her to wonder if it was one of Mrs. Miller's creations, but Sterling's jagged handwriting was lovingly dark against the crisp whiteness of the inside.

ELIZABETH, you have changed my life more than I can ever say. You have given me clarity. Direction. Ambition where I had none.

I know there is no making up for all my years wasted, all of the wealth I've just let flow away on petty things. How many people my family hurt without me ever knowing.

But I would like to try, starting with what you have left of your student loans. I have a check in my pocket that I would be honored to give to you, but I know enough about you to know that I need permission first.

So please, Elizabeth, let me take this step towards making my journey right.

She looked at the script that covered basically the whole inside of the card. Reading it once. Reading it twice. When she looked back to Sterling, he seemed uncertain, his brows furrowed as he watched her.

"That's too much to ask of you," she said, her eyes watering. He'd already bought her a whole *car*. That was probably worth five times more than her student loans, and yet he wanted to give her *more*.

She was well aware of his father's suspicions of her being a gold digger. She was also aware that was exactly what many of his rich acquaintances thought when they saw them together. And while she ignored each and every one of those people, she always wanted to make sure that Sterling never felt like he was being used for his money. Because she sincerely did *not* care if he was rich or not. Sure, it was *real* nice, but she had always been able to take care of herself.

"It isn't," he said, gently pulling her to him yet again.

It seemed that whenever they were together, they never liked to be more than a few inches apart. But she didn't mind. She didn't mind at *all*.

Sterling continued, "I just want you to have the same clean slate that I got to start with. It only seems fair, right?"

Part of her wanted to disagree, that stubborn and head-strong part of her that insisted upon forging her own path. But most of her was just so caught up in how *good* he was. So much different from the man that Teddy had described.

"If you say so," she murmured, unable to stop a few tears leaking from her eyes before she was up on her tiptoes again.

Their lips crashed together, so much emotion in their kiss that it left her breathless and hazy.

"Is that a yes?" he asked when she pulled back for a moment lest her heart explode.

"*Yes*," she whispered before kissing him once more. And maybe a couple more times. Just for good measure.

Sure, their future was still being built together, and things were up in the air, but she was absolutely certain that she had gotten luckier than she had ever dreamed of.

And goodness knew, her dreams were quite expansive.

EPILOGUE

Six Months Later

Sterling

"*H*ey, Silas, can I have a word with you?" Sterling asked.

"Right now?" his twin asked, looking uncertainly over his shoulder as the rest of his family filed into the arena.

"Yeah, it'll only take a minute and Teddy n' Elizabeth will watch our seats. Right, ladies?"

Teddy hummed her agreement, but Frenchie already had her arm looped around Elizabeth and was happily telling the woman all about the feral cat colony she was helping a rescue organization with. That seemed to be enough of a sign for Silas, however, and he peeled off with his brother.

"What's up?" he asked, looking confused.

Sterling couldn't exactly blame him. They were at their brother's graduation ceremony, which had been delayed a year because lil' Simon had decided to tack on his Master's degree, adding summer courses plus two semesters. He was completing his college career with honors. That was more than even Solomon did, although their second oldest brother had been pulled away from his studies to "learn the business" as it were. Sterling was pretty sure his father regretted that decision, considering that Solomon was the figurehead of the current rebellion they had going on.

"So, I realize this may not be the time, or the place, but with how often we've both been busy, I didn't want to put it off any longer."

"...uh-huh?"

Sterling felt his hands doing that thing where they started to gesture too much because he didn't know what to do with them. Shoving them into his pockets, he tried to look his twin in the eye. "Look, when we were kids, you got really hurt because of me. Permanently scarred. And I've never really apologized for it. Not *really*. And I want you to know, I am sorry. I really, *really* am."

Silas looked like he didn't know if he wanted to laugh or frown, and it came out as a confused sort of huff. "Sterling, we were teenagers—"

"That's what I've told myself for a long time to never take responsibility for it. But the fact is that you've been covering for me for most of our lives. I did something reckless; I did something that I wanted to do without any consideration for anybody else's health. You suffered the consequences for that.

"So, I wanted to tell you, I understand what I did was wrong. And even though it wasn't purposeful, I'm still responsible for something that affects you to this day. I realize that I've been selfish for a long, long time. But I hope you can tell I'm trying to be better."

"Sterling..." Silas looked like he might have had more to say, but instead he just strode forward and grabbed his younger twin in a hug.

Sterling embraced him back, nearly crushing his twin to him.

It felt *good,* even if he still felt plenty of shame for the past twelve years or so he'd spent pretending that he was fine. Maybe that was when the gap between them started, Silas permanently scarred by Sterling's actions and the reminder written right there in the older twin's flesh.

But where it had started didn't really matter. What mattered was that Sterling was working to close it, even if sometimes he felt like he had no idea what he was doing. His father certainly didn't help.

"Thanks, brother," Silas said when they parted, his eyes red and misty.

"Thank *you,*" Sterling answered. He thought of saying something snarky, something truly younger twin-ish, but he just didn't have it in him. He was still too emotional and raw.

"You ready to head back in now?"

"Sure. From what I saw in the program, it's gonna be a long production."

"Maybe we'll get lucky and Simon will be towards the front of the procession."

"Our name is *Miller*. He's probably going to be smack dab in the middle."

Silas let out a sigh. "Well, when you're right, you're right. But let's go support the squirt, shall we?"

"After you."

They headed into the arena and it was easy to find the

chunk that their whole family took up. At least two dozen of their cousins from Dad's three brothers were there, including Bart and Missy.

Now *she* was a classic bombshell if Sterling ever saw one, blond hair and all, and he didn't miss the awful looks that father and some other well-to-do folks gave her. But that didn't matter in the slightest because as soon as Missy and Elizabeth had crossed paths, it was like two halves meeting. He could see from where he was that his girlfriend had broken away from her conversation with Frenchie, only to be deeply involved in whatever she and Missy were discussing, the pair right next to each other. Bart, for what it was worth, looked thoroughly amused by the two.

"This should be fun," Sterling said, heading up the stairs to join them.

THE GRADUATION CEREMONY turned out to be lovely, not that Sterling expected anything less, if not a bit overdrawn. By the time it was over, everyone was hungry, and they were all taking their various vehicles to the restaurant they'd basically rented out.

"Why didn't you tell me you had a cousin-in-law that ran her own rescue?" Elizabeth said almost the exact moment she was in his truck, leveling an accusatory glare at him.

"Must have slipped my mind," he said with a smirk, carefully pulling out of his spot.

"Sure it did. You were just afraid that if we ever met each other, that we would be too powerful."

"And am I right in that assumption? Pretty sure I might

have heard plans for world domination for the sake of kittens in the middle of that graduation ceremony."

"You keep that to yourself," she responded primly as she settled in. "It'd be a shame to lose that pretty face."

"Oh, so you'd get rid of me for the sake of your evil plans?"

"No, I'd have to deal with you for the sake of the *kittens*, Sterling. It's all about scope."

He laughed, because how could he not? Usually only Silas got his sense of humor, but he could always count on Elizabeth understanding and giving it right back to him.

"Alright, well try to hold off on your plotting during my brother's party."

"I make no promises so that I might break no vows."

"*Uh-huh.*"

Sterling was indeed worried about the dinner. Such a large group of his family hadn't been gathered since his cousin Ben's wedding, and the tensions were running high. Very high. Especially considering that Samuel and his lovely lady—who apparently was another blond bombshell, was there something in the water up where they lived?—had chosen not to come so that they didn't take any attention away from Simon's big day.

While Sterling accepted and understood their reasoning, considering that their father certainly would have said one, two, or maybe a whole lot of nasty and unwelcome things, he still wished it didn't have to be that way. He missed his eldest brother, the softy of their line. He was the guy they all went to when they were down, and he wished that he hadn't spent so many years disparaging his brother's worth.

But there was time to make up for that in the future. Or at least he hoped so. First, they had to deal with the fight they had going on with their dad. Sal was very much *not* on board at all, and in fact, he seemed to be trying to gear himself up to take Solomon's place in the company.

...then again, hadn't Sterling—for a moment there—thought the same thing before he met Elizabeth?

Maybe his younger brother needed a slightly younger veterinarian to pop out of the ether and set him straight too. But Sterling was pretty sure that someone like that was a one of a kind thing, and he certainly wasn't giving up the love of his life.

Because, in the end, that was what Elizabeth was. He knew it right down to his bones. They'd come to know each other well in their year of being together, and he knew there would never be another for him. God had definitely set her in his path, and he wasn't going to ever let go.

But family drama and true love aside, they made it to the restaurant without incident. Elizabeth seemed to have gotten more comfortable with the expensive places that he and his family liked to frequent, but he didn't miss the way that her eyes widened when she saw the place.

"Wow," she whispered as he helped her out of the car.

"I know. But it'll be just us."

Her eyes flitted behind him, no doubt to the dozens of cars also in the parking lot. "'Just us' happens to include a whole lot of people, you know."

"Oh boy, am I aware."

And that was that, the two of them headed in. He wasn't sure who arranged the seating, but he was pleased that most of the people were pretty separated by who they got along with. That would certainly help.

They were family, sure, but Sal could be a little... *much* sometimes, and sometimes Bart could be sensitive. Something about his PTSD? Sterling wasn't sure. And then there was

Dad's general sour disposition and Mom's crumpled expression that always clouded her face anytime he fought with any of their sons.

Unfortunately, the main table was Simon, all of his brothers —minus Samuel—their partners and of course Mom and Dad. That itself was full of its own tension, but he just hoped that they could all behave.

Thankfully, the serving staff was on point. There'd been discussion of a buffet sort of setup, which Simon was perfectly fine with, but Father had refused, stating that buffets were low-class. They'd all chosen not to argue with him, as there were better fights to expend their energy on.

"Thank you all for gathering for me today," Simon said, standing up after everyone's drinks had been delivered and their orders taken.

Sterling was proud of his little brother, the actual runt of the family. Sure, he was still as muscled as one might expect an active Miller, but he was the shortest and slightest of them. In fact, he often reminded Sterling of their cousin Benji, the middle child of his set of cousins, all brothers.

But slight or not, Simon had managed to do what none of them had, subtly broken away, going to college to do his own thing. He had a good head on his shoulders, even if he didn't seem to have a set path, but at least he didn't have to run off with a woman to distance himself from their father's tight grip.

"I'm sure you all know that I've spent a lot of time working at college to make sure the investment in my education is worthwhile. I thank everyone who's given me support through this time, from Christmas cards to letters." He pointed over to Missy. "As well as successful tips on hiding a hamster in my dorm junior year."

"What?" Dad asked, cutting in.

Simon just continued right on. That was impressive. Sterling wasn't sure he had the *chutzpah* to ignore father like that.

"But the one thing that I have learned from all my expensive education is just how much I don't know. I've been taught so much, but we're all from the same little bubble. I want to know more of the world, all of its colors, cultures and shades. I feel like there's this whole wealth of knowledge that I can't find no matter how much I pay a school."

Interesting, but Sterling didn't really know where he was going with it. But Elizabeth was leaning forward on her elbows, watching Simon with a hawkish expression. It was one of the ones she only wore when something very important was happening, even if no one else was aware of exactly what was going on.

"And that is why I've decided to journey through Europe for the next six months. I have a guide picked out, and I've been training in what little free time I have. This isn't a lark, but something I've wanted to do since I got my BA. Now that I have my masters, I really don't have a reason not to.

"So, it's with all of you, my family, that I wanted a toast to the future! And wherever it takes us."

"You *what?*" Dad snapped, jumping up as quickly as a man of his age could.

"Honey," Mom said, gently gripping his arm, but Father shook her off.

"And you didn't think to talk about this with your *family?*" Dad thundered.

"I am talking about this with my family," Simon said serenely, looking straight ahead. "Am I not?"

"Yeah, what's this?" Sal parroted, because of course he did. "You trying to ditch your family like Sammy?"

"You *cut off* Sammy," Bart growled from another table. Sterling hadn't been expecting that, but Sal's gaze cut right to the burly man.

It was like the clashing of two giants. Of all the family, Bart was the biggest, but Sal was a close second, laden with muscle and a hot temper. Not exactly the best mixture. Sure, he was generally laid back, but when something did get under his skin, it went *deep*.

"What did you say, cousin?"

Missy's arm was on Bart's shoulder, her red lips whispering something into his ear. Bart clenched his drink, but otherwise his posture remained relaxed. "You practically chased Samuel out. Don't blame him for wanting to stay someplace he's loved."

"Oh *loved*, yes, because it's just some hippie commune up there," Dad snapped.

Sterling felt anxiety coiling in his gut. He didn't want the fight, but everything was unraveling so fast around him that he didn't know what to do.

Dad continued spewing, "And it has nothing to do with that floozy who—"

Wrong thing to say because then Missy was on her feet. In that flash of movement, Sterling was so reminded of Elizabeth that it was quite uncanny. What was it about the women who loved animals that made them so strong, so ready to throw down to protect the ones they loved?

"You say one bad thing about Virginia, I absolutely *dare* you," Missy said.

Dad looked surprised by the strange woman standing up to him, and Sterling took that as a moment to cut in.

"Look, *Dad*—"

"I don't need to hear anything from *you*," he snapped just as quickly, his eyes flicking to Sterling for only a moment. "Why would I listen to a son that's clearly just waiting for my death?"

"Hey, now!" Silas said, pushing himself back from the table with enough force for all of their silverware to shake.

"*Now, dear—*" Mom said, putting her hand on Dad's arm.

"You know what?" said one of Sterling's girl cousins from the west, a hard-as-nails type who he'd heard speak a grand total of twice in his life. "You spend so much time bullying everyone, you ever thought your own son wanted to get away from you just so he could breathe a little?"

Dad turned bright red at that, and it was very clear that there was no repairing the situation. Simon sat calmly, sipping his drink and happily eating a cheesy biscuit. Sterling didn't know where his youngest brother got his nonchalance, but he himself was sorely in need of some.

That was when a hand alighted on his elbow. He jerked in surprise before realizing it was Elizabeth, tugging on his sleeve. He shot her a stressed, curious expression, and her eyes shuttled to the door that was just a bit behind them and then back to him.

Oh. He got her point. And maybe it was cowardice, but he wanted to get away from the maelstrom behind him. It brought him no peace and just reminded him of all the avarice and resentment his branch of the family was putting into the world.

He nodded and then they were flitting out, nobody seeming to notice against the growing argument. They ended up outside, and the cool evening air was a blessing against his skin.

Turning to Elizabeth, he was completely ready to apologize, but stopped when he saw she was chuckling ever so lightly.

"What?" he asked, sighing in relief. Trust Elizabeth to take the bite out of such an awful situation.

"Oh, nothing." She smiled and crossed to him, her arms circling his neck. "I just thought that I had gotten used to the antics that came along with having a large family. But I suppose there's always something new to experience."

She was trying to comfort him, he knew that, but something about her word choice made his heart skip a beat. "Do you mean that?"

There was that cute little head tilt she did whenever she was trying to glean more information. "What do you mean?"

He swallowed, each of his words, feeling like they carried their own weight. "That you're getting used to us. As family?"

"Well, yeah. I would say we're practically family already, right? It certainly feels like it."

Oh, *oh*. Did she have any idea of what she was saying? Sterling thought probably not, but then again... with the way she was looking at him, it was hard not to feel like he just might be the center of the whole entire universe.

"Yeah, it does," he said. He couldn't resist anymore, he dipped his head down, claiming her mouth in his. His hands went about her waist. And like usual, he was flooded with heat and desire and more love than he thought it was possible for a single body to contain.

She was his salve, a balm for his soul. His teacher, his friend. She made him better in every way possible. He never wanted to be without her, no matter what that meant for his family and their fortune.

When their kiss broke, he didn't let go of her. No, instead he let his forehead rest against hers, looking into those perfect, deep eyes of hers. Eyes that saw the worst in him but still found a way to love him.

"What if we really did become a family?"

"I don't—"

But then he was reaching into his pocket, pulling out a small box. He'd had it ever since she had agreed to be his girlfriend and had kept it on him for when the time would feel right. And he couldn't imagine a moment more right than the one they were in.

The sun was setting behind Elizabeth, illuminating her in the delicate tendrils of coral and gold, shining along her dark skin like a seal of approval from God himself. And the way she was looking at him? It made his toes curl and his heart pound. Made him want to climb a mountain and scream of his love for her. Made him want to go around and smack anyone who dared do anything to hurt her or besmirch her name.

Except he didn't do any of those things. Instead, he knelt, flicking the box open with a finger to reveal a jeweled band.

"Elizabeth, I love you more than I can ever hope to say. But I hope you see it in my actions every day."

"This... this can't be happening," she said, hands going to her mouth. "Did you plan this?"

He shook his head. "No. Just been waiting for the right time, and I'm sure hoping this is it." Taking a deep breath, and then another, he affixed her with his steadiest gaze. "Elizabeth Brown, will you do me the honor of marrying me and having to deal with my crazy, dramatic family for the rest of our lives?"

It was like the moment after lasted an eternity. On one hand, he was absolutely certain that she would say yes. How could their love be so good if she didn't feel the same as him? But at the same time, there was that little insecure voice that said he wasn't good enough and that he never would be good enough. He would always be the younger twin. The middle child. About as useless as the junk drawer in the kitchen.

But then Elizabeth was speaking, and all the darkness was chased away. "Of course! Yes, absolutely, positively, *yes!*"

And just like that, he was soaring, flying higher than he ever thought possible. Slipping the ring onto her finger, he shot up and then they were kissing again. Naturally he had to spin her around, and she only protested a little.

"Do we need to get back inside?" Elizabeth asked.

"No way," he said. "I've finally found the love of my life and I just want to bask in this moment, just the two of us."

"That sounds perfect to me." She kissed him again.

He was going to have her lipstick all over his mouth, but he couldn't care less.

"I'm so happy you came into my life," he said between tender kisses. "You are perfect exactly as you are."

That must have been the right thing to say. Elizabeth's eyes misted over, and she wrapped her arms around him tighter.

Sterling held her, kissed her, hoped that she could feel how every single cell in his body was as in love with her as physically possible. And he took solace in knowing that no matter what happened with his family, their love was true.

It was a confusing, crazy time on the ranch, but he could always look to her for direction and what was important. Just as they'd found each other that one summer day, together they would find their way.

He was sure of that.

~

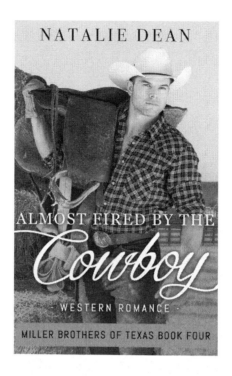

HELLO READER! I hope you enjoyed Sterling and Elizabeth's love story. It's time for the next handsome Miller brother! Salvatore and Nova have one of my favorite meeting scenes. She just started a new job on the ranch as a vet tech. Nova sees Sal about to kill an innocent snake and she all but tackles him to stop him from going through with it. He fires her on the spot but Elizabeth talks him out of it and it goes from there.

You can find Salvatore and Nova's love story on all major retailers. However, I'd be more than happy if you chose to buy it from my own small online business. Scan the QR code below to be taken to Almost Fired by the Cowboy at Natalie Dean Books. If scanning QR codes isn't your thing, you can also find my store here: nataliedeanbooks.com

ABOUT THE AUTHOR

Born and raised in a small coastal town in the south, I was raised to treasure family and love the Lord. I'm a dedicated homeschooling mom who loves to travel and spend time with my growing-up-too-fast son.

When I'm not busy writing or running my business, you can find me cleaning house, cooking dinner, feeding our three rescue cats, trying to make learning fun and coaxing my son to pick up his toys. On less busy days, you may also find me paddling down a spring run in Florida, hiking a mountain trail in Georgia (on the rare vacation to the mountains), or enjoying a book.

If you love Natalie Dean books, you can be notified of new releases by signing up to my newsletter at nataliedeanau thor.com, where you will also receive two free short stories for signing up. Just click on the "Free Books" tab at the top and you'll be on your way!

Also, as previously mentioned, I've opened my own online bookstore and I'd love your support! As of June 2024, I'm selling my ebooks at Natalie Dean Books. By late summer or fall 2024, I should have audiobooks, regular paperbacks, large print paperbacks, dyslexic print paperbacks and signed paper-backs all available. At the request of my loyal readers, I'll also be adding merchandise, such as glasses, cups, magnets and more. So come check out my small mom-owned author busi-ness at nataliedeanbooks.com.

You can also scan the QR code below to be taken to the home page of Natalie Dean Books.

f facebook.com/nataliedeanromance